About the Author

Tony George (as Roger A. Beamish) is a first-time author of this crime mystery story. Its genesis comes from the author's decades-long interest in detectives and crime, especially gothic and film noir themes, together with all the film and television detective productions from the 1940s until the present. Favourites are too numerous to mention but they begin from the gothic novels of the nineteenth century and run through the golden age of crime novels in the 1920s and 1930s, then on to film noir and television detectives such as

Columbo, Poirot and Marple, Morse, Vera, Wallander, Endeavour, and so on. He received his doctorate at Sydney University and postdoctoral fellowships at Tufts Medical School, Boston, and the John Curtin Medical School at the Australian National University. He is presently an associate professor in the School of Life Sciences at the University of Technology Sydney.

Inspector Dillon and The Case of the Missing Girl

Roger A. Beamish

Inspector Dillon and The
Case of the Missing Girl

Vanguard Press

VANGUARD PAPERBACK

© Copyright 2024
Roger A. Beamish

The right of Roger A. Beamish to be identified as author of this work has been asserted by him in accordance with the Copyright, Designs and Patents Act 1988.

All Rights Reserved

No reproduction, copy or transmission of this publication may be made without written permission.
No paragraph of this publication may be reproduced, copied or transmitted save with the written permission of the publisher, or in accordance with the provisions of the Copyright Act 1956 (as amended).

Any person who commits any unauthorised act in relation to this publication may be liable to criminal prosecution and civil claims for damages.

A CIP catalogue record for this title is available from the British Library.

ISBN 978 1 80016 852 7

This is a work of fiction. Names, characters, businesses, places, events and incidents are either the product of the author's imagination or used in a fictitious manner. Any resemblance to actual persons, living or dead, or actual events is purely coincidental.

Vanguard Press is an imprint of
Pegasus Elliot Mackenzie Publishers Ltd.
www.pegasuspublishers.com

First Published in 2024

Vanguard Press
Sheraton House Castle Park
Cambridge England

Printed & Bound in Great Britain

Dedication

Rose, Antony Jess, Tim, Molly, Olive, Elliot, Phoebe, Henry, Lavina, Vince, Tony, Evelyn, Paul, Zahia

CHAPTER 1
Puzzle

Have you ever walked alone in an old cemetery at night? Dark, eerie, ghostly, and nightmarish, are just a few words to describe such an excursion. It's often pitch black, the leaves rustle in the trees and the dappled starlight seen through the leaves increases the sense of fear. If the moon is about then its ghostly light is just enough to make things even creepier. Rows of cold headstones of long-ago living persons make the mostly noiseless atmosphere forbidding. Dim shafts of light send shivers down the spine as they suggest movement, or is it a trick of the mind? If you have just entered the front gates, then the dread and foreboding haven't hit you yet and it's simple enough to turn around and go away. But if you do manage to venture in among the gravestones, then all the fears just described begin to register and terror takes hold of the senses. In broad daylight, the same place is neither menacing nor frightening.

So, what was Charles Fitzroy Keane doing alone in a Muirford cemetery on that cold moonless night on the

15 April 1950? He was clad in a mackintosh and rainhat against a fierce Atlantic rain squall saturating the rocky bluff on which the cemetery stood, in the yard of the small gothic St Mark's church in this remote outpost in West Cornwall. The wind was terrific in its intensity and the rain hurt as the propelled droplets hit Keane's face. Shafts of lightning lit up the stained glass of the old church. The trees groaned with the wind and rain, and their dead branches swayed and creaked and assumed odd creepy shapes when lit by lightning flashes.

The sodden headstones were like dark dull mirrors amid the shadow cast by the old church. No living soul about, just dark and light, soaking windswept rain and Keane fighting the elements as he used his torch to examine each of the thirty or so headstones in the dim night light. Now and then he started, even jumped from the odd mix of noises that conjured in his mind images of someone else present, a person, an apparition? He stopped, squinted, and read the epitaph on one of the headstones:

Daddy, I think I'll have a little sleep. Here lies Daphne Welles, only child of William and Caroline Welles, taken aged sixteen on the Eleventh Day of March 1948 AD.

Charles Fitzroy Keane had found what he was looking for and fixed the words in his memory.

Charles walked heavily and quickly back to his car and drove the two miles to the village and the warmth and comfort of his room at the local inn. Well, might you ask, why did he drive out to the cemetery in such inclement weather and at night? Why not during that day, or the next day? Was he trying to avoid being seen on his trip to find Daphne's grave on such a night as this? Will we find the answers to these questions?

The next morning, the maid brought Keane's breakfast tray to his room. She knocked twice on the door but there was no response, so she entered and found, to her horror, a "sleeping" corpse in the bed with blood saturating his pyjama top. Charles Fitzroy Keane had died during the night, killed by the hand of he who was on the same quest for the name on the headstone. The "secret" text had perished with the death of Fitzroy Keane, murdered in his bed, and it seemed that the words inscribed on the headstone were fated to go with him to his grave.

The local constabulary was called to the inn and began taking particulars and photos as is customary, but their notes would not record the events of the previous night at St Mark's cemetery. There were no identification papers on the body so all they had to go on was the name he had written in the inn's register, Charles Fitzroy Keane, alongside which he also scribbled his address as Massinone, Midlands. The only item of note that the police found was a tightly crumpled piece of paper, formed into a small ball, and lodged into the toe of one of his shoes left alongside the bed. When the paper was unfurled and flattened out on the small table under a wall mirror, what the police saw was not the text on Daphne Welles's headstone, but a puzzle that made no sense to those who looked at it. Was it a clue to the murderer or some other intrigue that had the police tilting at windmills that morning? Upon returning to the small police station, the local sergeant in charge, who was also unable to make any sense of the scrap of paper, sent it off to New Scotland Yard in London.

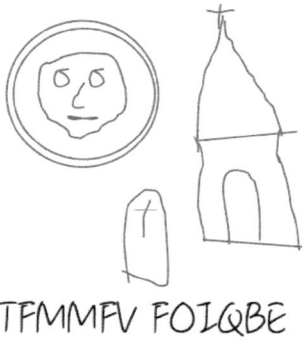

TFMMFV FOLQBE

Chief Superintendent Douglas Sinclair decided that this bit of remote flummery did not deserve heavy resources or any of his best detectives, so he summoned Inspector James Wilson-Smythe, still inexperienced but making his way up the ladder. Wilson-Smythe reminded the Chief Super that he was still working on the Tottenham Corner robbery which should be concluded in a week or so and he would be happy to join the case then. Light flummery it might be, but it would not do to ignore it for a week or more, as the press would be baying for news. The Super had to act and called for the newly appointed Detective Inspector Harry Dillon.

'Dillon, you are new here and I'd like to get you off to a good start by assigning you your own case. Here's the file, it's a murder in some God-forsaken village in West Cornwall. It seems like the victim had no known relatives or past life for that matter. His address in the hotel register gives Massinone in the Midlands as his home. But you know what, there is no such place in all of Great Britain!'

The Super handed him the scrap of paper bearing a puzzle drawn by the victim. 'Now there's a tricky little mystery for you to spend a couple of weeks on. Naturally, this puzzle will not be released to the newspapers until we get it figured out, and maybe not even then. Let me know how you go.'

When Dillon settled at his desk, with a cup of tea and biscuit for his morning break, he had before him a distinctly odd puzzle on a scrap of paper, a dead man, and no knowledge of how the puzzle might be connected with the victim's trip to the cemetery. Only the victim knew the solution to the puzzle, and he had left it seemingly as a clue to be deciphered in the event of his death, which clearly, he had expected as a strong possibility. Harry surmised that the puzzle was at least an inkling as to the reason for the secrecy surrounding Keane's late-night visit to the clifftop cemetery in such inclement weather. He was trying to outwit the person following him and it seems he succeeded in that endeavour at the cemetery, but alas, not in preserving his life that night back at the inn. Dillon was not about to make wild assumptions. At Scotland Yard, you are taught to gather the facts, interpret, and analyse the evidence then come up with the best route to the detective's gospel: means, motive, opportunity.

Inspector Dillon gazed at the puzzle for perhaps five minutes but could make nothing of it. He called in other officers and then a couple of more seasoned detectives, none of whom could tell him anything other than whatever was held in the cryptic message no doubt occurred at Muirford — a person, a church, a gravesite, a name? His colleagues, and he included himself in this assessment, were about as helpful as a cup of cold porridge!

Harry Dillon was twenty-six, well-educated, reasonably worldly in matters social and professional. He was of average height, lean, roughly handsome, and a little swarthy from his Celtic roots. He fancied himself clever, especially following his recent promotion to inspector, but this puzzle had him stumped. He had heard about killers or victims leaving cryptic messages at a crime scene, either displayed openly or hidden as in this case.

The next day, Dillon drove up to Oxford. He was a good learner and judge of character, so his task this day was to seek help from an "acquaintance" at Oxford. He knocked at a modest cottage just off Banbury Road. His sister opened the door.

'Hi, sis, thought I'd drop in for the weekend.'

'Harry, you know you are always welcome, after all, it *is* your house that you let me subsist in rent-free while I am studying.'

'Think nothing of it, just thought it a good idea to visit and catch up on local gossip. How about lunch, then a bit of a walk around Oxford?'

Milly Dillon was a very attractive twenty-three and an archivist researcher on the urbanization of London; a task she was studying for her doctorate at St Anne's College. Her research had her spending most of her daily hours at the Bodleian Library. Milly was fairer than her brother, comely, with shoulder-length light auburn hair, freckles, and a very winning smile.

Harry loved the little cottage, but his career in London had to come first, and he was pleased to help his 'little' sister who lacked income while pursuing her doctorate. The cottage was bought by their parents for their elder son, Liam, who joined the RAF in early 1940 and was shot down and killed during the "Battle of Britain." Harry had always felt guilty about inheriting the cottage from his dead brother, but that's how things were sorted, and he didn't mind Milly getting most of the benefit. Harry had tried to enlist but was overlooked; poor hearing was the reason, so he stayed with his studies and earned a little money as one of a small group helping to draw battlefield maps.

Dressed in casual wear, brother and sister engaged in small banter and local gossip while they prepared sandwiches and a pot of tea. At the table, Milly asked her brother,

'Any interesting cases yet?'

'Funny you should say that sis! I want you to turn your talents to a little puzzle I have inherited in my first murder case.'

Milly beamed like a little child about to be given a treat. Harry related the main particulars to his sister, then took out the scrap of paper and pressed it down on the table for her to see.

'I showed it to a few detectives at the Yard, but like me, none could make head nor tail out of it, other than the obvious drawings. Charles Fitzroy Keane must have scratched this drawing to hide the clue he'd found at the cemetery from his pursuer who killed him but failed to find this piece of paper, which was recovered from the toe of one of the victim's boots.'

Milly summoned all her intrigue and interest and pored over the puzzle for some minutes. Then she announced, 'You must have divined that the figure on the left is a man, possibly bespectacled, alongside what looks like a church and a grave and a name, possibly of the man, or the person buried there?'

'Yes, easy enough to figure that far but at the Yard we were all side-tracked by the odd arrangement of letters in the name and became totally confused. You will have guessed now that the puzzle is the reason for this visit, but I was planning to see my dear sister anyway so, here we are, and since you were always cleverer than me, it's all yours!'

'Harry, it's always good to see you, no matter the reason, and the spare room is always made up ready for your flying visits. Now let's take a closer look at this conundrum. A man at a church and a name, a man's name, or a woman's? Looks like a jumbled anagram of sorts, but as you say, the letters make no sense. In fact, the first name has no vowels, so there's a puzzle all of its own! Let's think about it on our walk.'

They struck out from the cottage towards town, around The Covered Market, and onto the High Street, down Magpie Lane, and behind Merton College onto the prophetically named "Dead Man's Walk." Behind them was the Merton College tower and ahead and to the left, the higher tower at Magdalen College. Indeed, Oxford is one of those glorious places where you can walk in and out of colleges, shops, museums, parks, and houses, all sharing space around mostly the High Street, the Broad and Banbury Road, and down to the river Cherwell, which joins the Thames at Oxford. Harry had studied here for three years, so knew it well. There was the New Theatre, which tried out concerts and such before they went on to London, and the many pubs, where ale, pork pies, and football were the main fare.

Settling on a bench, Milly summed up to her brother where she was at with the puzzle,

'Harry, the man in the picture has a double ring around his head.'

'Yes, I wondered whether that was significant,' said Harry.

Milly continued, 'Well, walking now past all these colleges and churches, could it be a halo, and could he be a saint?'

'That's good, sis, and the church alongside, what do you make of it?'

'Tell me, brother, are there any churches in Muirford village?'

'Yes, of course, two of them. St Barnabas in the village and St Mark's on a rocky bluff with an old cemetery in its church yard.'

'Well, that's it, Harry, it has to be St Mark's! That's the clue of the man with the halo, he represents St Mark, and the encrypted name in the puzzle must be someone buried in that cemetery.'

'I think you are on to something, sis, but what about the odd first name without a vowel?'

Milly thought and thought and came back with, 'Could it be Welsh? They have many such words for people and places in Wales.'

'Now that's good thinking. Let's call it quits for now and enjoy the rest of the weekend sightseeing until I leave tomorrow afternoon.'

'Fine, Harry, but what about the mystery name?'

'Easy, sis, you are going to check up on all Welsh or any other country's first names at the Bodleian Library this coming week and send on your searches to me at the Yard. It's a start and where better to look up names than here at the Bodleian?'

'Thanks, brother, and do you expect me to feed you for the rest of this weekend? Just joking, I'm becoming as interested in this murder as you are. Maybe we can surprise your Chief Superintendent at Scotland Yard. He might even give your report card a gold star?'

'We'll see,' said Harry, his gaze off into the distance at the many college spires trying to reach the low-lying clouds floating by.

He and Milly loved this city and the little cottage. Their parents had stayed behind in their native Belfast but purchased the cottage for elder son, Liam. Milly and Harry followed him to England, now their home. It was easier for young people to study and work here than in Ireland and they were making rewarding efforts that were comforting to their parents.

CHAPTER 2
Wilcote Hall

A week later, London was enjoying a rare sun-drenched day and Harry Dillon was just about to indulge in morning tea, bathing in the sun's rays streaming through the window behind his desk, when the post arrived. There was a letter from Milly which he eagerly tore open and read the words on the single page: "Dear brother, hours of research and consulted a language expert at Balliol College with the grand conclusion that there are no such names in the Welsh or any other language! Your loving sis, Milly. PS We should meet up to discuss what to do next."

One of Harry's fellow detectives was from a wealthy family who lived on a small estate just outside Oxford, near Woodstock. Detective Inspector James Wilson-Smythe had been offered the case by the Chief Super but had to decline while finishing his robbery brief. James' family lived at Wilcote Hall out beyond Blenheim Palace. James, or Jim as he liked to be known, had small digs in London but went to Wilcote most weekends to spend time with his parents, Richard and Helen, his older brother, Dexter, and two younger sisters, Kate and Lavinia. Jim was the same age as Harry, twenty-six, athletic, fair, and good-looking. His sisters were twenty-three and twenty. All were well-educated, of course. Dexter, now aged thirty, would inherit the estate as older brothers do, which explained Jim's more worldly profession as a detective.

Jim had got to know Harry and they often lunched together or had after-work drinks at the Old Crown just down the road from the Yard. Jim invited Harry to Wilcote Hall a few times these past months, but he declined each time as he needed his weekends to study the law and rules of being a detective in the plumiest police station of them all, and to visit his sister, Milly, on rare free weekends. Now that Harry had a perplexing case dumped in his lap, he planned to take up Jim's latest invite to Wilcote Hall and at drinks one evening, asked if Jim wouldn't mind his younger sister tagging along for the weekend.

Jim laughed, 'Harry, we have twelve bedrooms so I'm sure we can fit you and your little sister into two of the spare visitor suites. I have a few dinner jackets so no need to pack one. Actually, I'll put a suit in your wardrobe, so you'll always have it when you visit. Ditto for your sister. My Kate and Lavinia, like most girls these days, have more clothes than they can possibly wear.'

Harry told Jim that he had an ulterior motive in agreeing to spend the weekend at Wilcote Hall. He hoped that banging more heads together on this case might cough up a clue or two.

'Perfect idea, old man. The Chief Super offered me the case a couple of weeks ago, but I was busy with that Tottenham Corner robbery business. Maybe we could work together on this one?'

'Grand idea. Maybe the Chief Super will stick gold stars in both our files!'

Harry turned up at the cottage in Oxford early Saturday morning and announced to Milly that he had a surprise in store. They were going to spend the weekend at his colleague Jim's family estate out past Woodstock.

Milly was aghast, 'How could you be so insensitive, Harry? I have no formal clothes and neither do you for that matter and you expect us to go to high tea and dinner in rags!'

'Come on, sis, Jim is an easy-going guy, not an aristocratic bone in his body. I'm sure his sisters will find you an outfit or two to wear to high tea and high table. At least we have well-groomed table manners from back home!'

'Harry! You have no idea of a girl's needs. It's not just about clothes, it's about those uppity airs and graces, but you are serving us up as *disgraces*!'

'Oh, hang it, sis, you'll do very well. You are a cute little thing and I'm sure Jim and his folks will like you.'

'I'm sure his sisters are snotty stuck-up snobs with retroussé noses and prim-and-proper dowdy dresses with hair tied in tight buns. What would I care about being liked by snobs? It's just the embarrassment of it all.'

'So what! Now pack an overnight bag and out to the car and off we go!'

She went against her better judgement but continued to berate her brother during the short drive out to Wilcote Hall.

'There you go, nonchalantly smelling the breeze as you drive us to disgrace and doom!'

Harry turned towards her and said, 'Milly dear, there is an ulterior motive for this stayover. I am going to set our puzzle before the whole Wilson-Smythe clan and see if we can make some progress. Good idea, eh?'

'No, but it's too late now,' said Milly, as she sank back in the seat with a dull frown on her brow.

Harry drove up the estate driveway to the front of the hall. A footman appeared and welcomed them while attending to their small valises. Jim ran out to meet them, shaking Harry's hand vigorously but looking at Milly. Jim saw a cute little auburn-haired girl with freckles and a very becoming smile.

'So, Harry old man, this is your baby sister,' as he extended his hand to shake hers, gently and warmly.

Milly couldn't help noticing that Harry's friend was tall, handsome, and friendly, but in another class from their humble origins. She was used to seeing "commoner" versions of Jim almost every day back in Oxford.

'How do you do, Milly, and welcome to Wilcote Hall.'

'Very good of you to let Harry bring his *baby* sister along with him.'

Jim smiled at her little backhander as the three of them went up the stairs and into the hall.

'Morning tea is in the breakfast room in an hour and we will see you both there,' said Jim, breaking off to another wing of the house while the footman helped them to their rooms up on the first landing.

Milly and Harry sauntered casually into the breakfast room and Milly, at least, sensed quite a few pairs of eyes looking her up and down with varying smiles; from slight and probably forced by Jim's mother and elder son, Dexter, to broad by Richard, Kate and Lavinia, and Jim broadest of all. Dexter was typically close to his mother in looks and composure, while Jim's sisters were much more informally dressed, engagingly friendly and eager to make Milly feel welcome. They seemed everything but snotty, dowdy snobs. Both were very attractive, with hair allowed to run down to their shoulders, like her own. She looked more closely and saw that the older sister, Kate, was quite a beauty. They launched into a three-way separate conversational grouping, while the others engaged in the usual badinage that befits such informal visits. Well, thought Milly to herself, thanks to Jim's invitation and Harry's rush of blood acceptance, it might be an interesting visit after all, despite the trappings of wealth and social status. Milly was surprised at the informal friendliness and felt a little guilty for chiding Harry earlier.

After Jim's parents and Dexter had finished their interrogation of Harry, his and Milly's origins, their parents remaining in Ireland, schooling, and what each was doing now, the rest of the day went as country estate days are known to do. An informal light lunch, horse riding, walks in the gardens, more small talk, and finally, preparations for dinner, at which Milly was fortunate to have a wide choice of evening attire from Jim's sisters, who continued to fuss over her. Milly couldn't help but melt to their instant attention and warmth. The threesome went down to dinner looking pictures of loveliness and they were all congratulated on their winsome appearance. Jim continued his increasingly besotted attention to Milly.

When dinner was concluded, Jim announced the real reason for Harry and Milly's visit. The puzzle was produced from Harry's pocket and circulated among the Wilson-Smythes, who continued to pass it around as Milly explained what she and Harry knew about the church and jumbled name.

'Yes, I know Muirford. I visited there once or twice during the war,' offered Dexter, 'but I never ventured up to the old church and graveyard.'

'It's a thrilling mystery and I'm sure we will all have fun solving this puzzle and the murder,' Lavinia screeched gleefully.

'This is a dire and dark business,' Richard added soberly, 'and you two detectives should tread carefully.'

'Yes,' said Helen, 'and I'd feel much reassured, Jim, if you and Harry avoided danger in this endeavour.'

'It's not my case, mother,' replied Jim, 'I'm only the messenger and passenger. Maybe I could be Watson to Harry's Sherlock?'

'What fun!' Lavinia again, with all the exuberance of carefree youth.

Then Kate said something that made Harry look up, 'Messenger, passenger, or whatever, Jim, we are all in on it now. After you three drive back tomorrow, you must watch over each other so that no harm comes to any of you. There is a murderer out there, and heaven forbid, he happens upon you knowing about this puzzle.'

Kate continued, 'This is a bad business, as father has said, Jim, and what about young Milly here? I can't believe that you and Harry are treating this like one of those boys' own mystery adventures and ignoring Milly's wellbeing.'

Harry wanted to respond, tactfully, of course, but was beaten by Milly almost blurting out that she was aware of the danger but that by virtue of her studies she had an innate sense of investigative curiosity. She was sure that Harry and Jim would keep her and themselves out of harm's way.

Jim gulped and exclaimed quickly, 'Yes, of course, we will be looking after Milly.' That ended the conversation with most sensing Jim taking a protective "brotherly" concern for Milly. Kate continued to fix Harry and Jim with a stern look of disapproval.

Before retiring to their beds for the evening, copies of the cryptic name were made and given out to all present. They would compare notes and possible solutions to the jumbled letters the next day. Sunday almost passed without event, other than the trappings of country estate living; with meals, walks, and banter until mid-afternoon when the two detectives and Milly were to drive back to Oxford and London. No one had made any progress on the lettering, despite Lavinia filling several pages of attempted anagram solving!

Jim managed to be diverted by his attention to Milly and she was not displeased by it, except for her shyness, which shielded her from any serious reciprocity, knowing as she did how impossible such a union would be. She steeled herself from it but was warmed by the thought that she could go back to her studies dreaming at least of an impossible romantic "attachment" to her brother's new friend. Such dreamy play-acting would help while away the long days of study in Oxford.

Harry noticed his sister's reticence to talk and her staring into the distance on the trip back to Oxford. All he could get out of her by the time they bade each other farewell, was that she would keep trying to solve the puzzle. Then, just as he prepared to drive off, Milly spoke out.

'Harry, I don't like this turn of events. You have your job to do back in London yet here you are bringing this family into a murder case, no less! Didn't you get the sense that these Wilson-Smythes are afraid of their privacy being breached?'

'Oh, sis, you fuss too much. I'm sure it will all settle down and someone will be found soon to confess to that killing out at Muirford.'

CHAPTER 3
The "Oxford Four"

She was distant, surly, disinterested, uncommunicative, and cold, yet there was something in Kate Wilson-Smythe that made Harry dwell more on her than on the puzzle in the week that followed. He shouldn't be so distracted, but she *was* beautiful — slim and elegant and unattainable of course. He told himself, isn't it always so, the girl who was in another class in looks and in station. By Friday, he had just about taken the cure, freeing himself from these thoughts.

There were no exchanges of clues by the Wilcote Hall party. On the other hand, Jim managed to find a reason to write to Milly. He had taken to her cuteness and easy-going manners and was beginning to like her a lot, and she him, but she remained cool, and friendly, in her reply. After all, nothing usually comes out of a first meeting and she was sure it would all wear off in a week or so, but her dreaming could go on! Harry and Jim continued to meet occasionally for lunch or after-work drinks at the Old Crown, and at one such meeting, Jim mentioned that Kate was going up to Oxford to visit a friend on the weekend. He offered the chance that she might call on Milly if she wasn't pressed for time.

Harry thought that a kindly gesture were it to happen. He fixed himself on seeing Kate again, if only to divine if that exterior coolness went to the core of her being, or if there was a glimmer of warmth lurking in there somewhere. Jim had managed to put his sister back at the front of Harry's thoughts! Try as he might, he couldn't get her out of his mind.

Harry had liked other girls and went out with one or two for a while, but nothing came of those short match ups — the park, the cinema, lunches, dinners, kisses, and finally, detachment. Would he ever find a girl, *any* girl? Kate was anything but approachable, yet he was drawn to her and wondered if she could ever like him. Maybe her coolness was because she was engaged to a cousin, a neighbour or friend, not an uncommon situation in families with names and estates. He could ask Jim but didn't want to venture any interest, for fear of disappointment, or worse, of Jim letting Kate know that she had a new admirer. He would use the pretext of visiting Milly so went up to Oxford the next weekend hoping that he might bump into Kate at Milly's, or in the street, or somewhere, anywhere. He hated being devious, but he was curious, as detectives are apt to be!

When Harry arrived at the cottage on Saturday morning, he was surprised to be told by his sister that she, Kate, and Jim were meeting at noon at the nearby Melrose Inn to work on the puzzle. Jim hadn't mentioned this trip and Harry immediately realised that his friend was as devious as himself! Jim was using Kate and the puzzle as pretexts to spend time with Milly. This didn't really surprise Harry as Jim had spent most of his time last weekend at Wilcote Hall in deep conversation with his sister and so a budding romance was on the cards. Kate was to be the token chaperone for this Oxford meeting.

Before leaving the cottage to strike out for the Melrose Inn, Harry asked, 'Tell me, sis, are you falling for Jim?'

'What sort of a question is that Harry? How could I? You know that we are outsiders, and they are gentrified untouchables.'

'Just a thought, sis. I sense that he thinks you are sweet.'

'Sweet is easy but trying to fit into that family is distinctly unnerving. I think we should keep to our station and not be distracted by such interludes. Don't forget, we are Irish, not English! Let's concentrate on murder, not romance.'

When all four had gathered at the tavern, friendly conversation started up, lunch was ordered, and first drinks were brought to the table. Jim managed to sidestep Harry not being invited with a fallback in knowing that Milly was expecting him this weekend. Harry couldn't help noticing that Kate was still reticent and haughty, but she was animated and friendly with Milly.

'Now, down to business,' announced Jim.

All four produced their copies of the puzzle and scribbled odd bits of text on one or both sides of the paper. Harry, Milly, and Jim hadn't anything of real value, other than dallying with letter rearrangements, which went nowhere, but Kate surprised the others by having distilled the problem into a few questions, which she had jotted down on the back of her copy.

'One, who was Charles Fitzroy Keane?'

'Two, he gave his address as Massinone in the Midlands, but no such place exists so where did he come from to be in Muirford that night?'

'Three, the murderer was following Keane and killed him in his sleep. So, the killing, and not the puzzle or cemetery, was probably his main purpose. And yet, Keane went to a lot of trouble to disguise his visit to the cemetery. Why?'

'Four, who or what is Tfmmfv Foiqbe?'

'Five, what was the significance of the cemetery and church? Tfmmfv Foiqbe is probably buried there, going on the drawing of a gravestone above the name.'

'That's it in a nutshell, many questions, no answers. Is it worth our time to go on with this complicated cryptic mystery?'

'What! Of course it is, Kate,' said Jim in an animated voice. 'Have you no sense of daring and moral focus? This is Harry's work assignment and solving this murder could make his career at the Yard. And have you not noticed how Milly has thrown her own thoughts into this case to help her brother?'

'Yes, of course. When you put it that way. I'm sorry, Milly, but I did spend time summing up the issues of this mystery. Now I'm hoping it will go away.'

'No need to apologise, Kate,' said Milly, 'it's not your burden and no one would blame you for not taking any interest at all. Yet you've left us trailing badly behind your perceptive analysis.'

Lunch was almost finished when Milly came up with an idea. 'You know what, I have a friend at college whose brother worked as a cryptographer during the war at Bletchley Park, or one of those places. Why don't I have my friend pass the puzzle on to him?'

'Grand idea,' said Jim.

Harry nodded in agreement. 'This will give us some inkling of whether this weird name or place can be deciphered. But if he doesn't work it out, then we are in a real pickle *and* up a gum tree!'

'Well, there are other cryptographers, even crossword solvers we could seek out,' added Jim.

'Yes, of course, Jim. Dear sister, Milly, it's in your lap for a week. Why don't we all meet here next Saturday to see if anything comes of it?'

'Done, old man,' said Jim, rising from his chair. He, like Harry, liked the bit about meeting again at the Melrose Inn. The detectives could try to make further progress on their other "cases," the girls. Milly was pleased to have thought of the idea. Kate gave a typical nonchalant shrug of the shoulders.

The party broke up. Kate went off to meet her friend. Jim drove back to London. Harry went with Milly back to the cottage, and as soon as they went in and sat down, Milly couldn't help but say to her brother,

'She's beautiful, isn't she?'

'And doesn't she know it!'

'I was only saying it as an obvious fact. Look, Harry, boys like you don't usually fuss about looks, but for girls, especially ones that are not well-educated or ensconced in a profession, looks are everything. There are thousands of very attractive and pretty girls in England, but few that one can say are truly beautiful, and I'm simply saying that Kate is one of them.'

Harry chipped in, 'Botticelli's *Venus* is painted on canvas. The *Venus di Milo* is a marble statue. Both are beautiful, but unattainable to the hoi polloi.'

'Oh, Harry, you are too touchy. I was only saying that she is beautiful. I wasn't asking you to put her on a pedestal.'

They both laughed when Harry said the obvious, 'she is *already* on a pedestal; the problem is working out how to make her come down to mix with mere mortals like us!'

Later that afternoon, Harry went out to buy a newspaper and read it over tea and cake at a nearby café. He always scanned the obituary notices and this time found one for Charles Fitzroy Keane, recently deceased, no background notes or family mentioned, just dates and the place of burial.

Harry telephoned the newspaper, and after getting through to the relevant section, asked who had paid the burial costs and wrote the obituary. The newspaper clerk looked up the register and told Harry that the costs were paid by a member of parliament, a Mr William Brogan-Moore. Harry was startled, but still wondered whether this had any relevance to the case, or if it simply reflected the victim's circle of friends. Was it one of those red herrings that are found often enough in murder cases? Of course, it was a clue of sorts and had to be chased up.

On returning to the cottage, he showed the article to Milly, who asked intuitively, 'How does a London MP come to know the victim, who was murdered in his sleep at a nondescript village in West Cornwall, and whose origins are who-knows-where?'

'Mutual friends?' Harry offered.

'No, there is something sinister about this and it is no doubt connected to our still-nameless cemetery corpse in that grave!'

'You know, I see a few dead ends coming up and no easy solutions. Sis, sometimes I think you should be the detective in this family, and I should tend the garden here.'

'Oh, don't be self-deprecating Harry, we both know that you are clever, it's just that you haven't had a chance to apply your intellect to this mystery yet, but you will. Of that, I am in no doubt. How else would you have become a Detective Inspector at Scotland Yard?'

She went on, 'And yet, there is nothing wrong with using our "Group of Four," our "Oxford Four," to tackle this case with relish *and* enthusiasm! Let's see what comes of my friend's cryptographer passing his searching eye over the puzzle! Speaking of our "Oxford Four," isn't it intriguing that your friend, Jim, likes me, but I dare not reciprocate, and you like Kate, cold fish that she is, and who gives you not the slightest attention.'

'How delicately you put it, sister dear.'

She looked at him, pouted, and arched an eyebrow. They both laughed at the impossibility of it all and yet it still gave them a playful sense of fun. Outside, the birds flew and sang on the boughs of trees and roofs, the colleges' spires still reaching for the clouds. One could lose all sense of time here and drift and dream until real life disturbed the peace again.

CHAPTER 4
Daphne Welles

There is something about this case that looks bigger than a simple murder, sir,' said Harry to Chief Superintendent Sinclair, who was asking if any progress had been made. After detailing a list of a few very tenuous threads, plus Kate's questions, the obituary notice and William Brogan-Moore MP, Harry added that he had a cryptographer working on the odd name on the puzzle left by the victim. If that works out, then it could be a new lead.'

The Super braided his forehead at seeing this pup of a detective flailing in his first serious case. The last thing the Yard needed was an MP coming after them. It always spells trouble, and he told Harry as much, adding, 'Look, Dillon, why don't you compare your latest notes with Wilson-Smythe. Give it a week or so to see if you two can muster a new clue or two. Let's leave the MP alone for the present.'

'Thank you, sir, good idea, I'll get on with it today.'

Harry told Jim about the MP item he had found, but they both dismissed this for the present as being of no pressing importance or even relevance as far as they could see and trained their minds on the next meeting with the girls when Milly would give an accounting of the cryptographer's work of the jumbled name in the puzzle. This had to be the key to the mystery and the easiest path to finding the murderer, or at least a promising way forward.

Saturday morning came and the group assembled once more at the Melrose in Oxford. A bright day outside, drinks and small talk inside. Harry tried asking Kate a few nondescript questions and her answers were mostly monosyllabic, so he gave up after a few minutes. He and Jim started up a conversation and during it, Harry couldn't help but notice Kate stealing little expressionless glances in his direction. Was she being dismissive of this gauche commoner, or was this her usual manner, to stare but not to commit or comment? At his wits' end to figure it out, he let it go.

Milly was the last to arrive, as she had been at the Bodleian. She smiled knowingly at the others as she took her seat and a sip of her wine. She reached into her small briefcase and produced a piece of paper and laid it out on the table. They saw three rows of hand-printed letters, thus:

TFMMFV FOIQBE
SELLEW ENHPAD
DAPHNE WELLES

'The cryptographer had solved the name puzzle in just ten minutes,' Milly announced with glee.

'It's no wonder we won the war,' said Jim, as he, like the others, zoomed in on the third row, which spelt out finally what they had sought.

As recounted by Milly, the puzzle solver told her friend that he had worked out that it was a simple one-letter transposition —— simple to him that is, Milly said. He tried a few things but then saw the correct organisation of the letters once he figured that the lettering could be back to front *and* transposed. It was a simple trick used in early code writing. The transposed lettering is shown on the second line and the reversed letters on the third. "Daphne Welles" had emerged from the dead man's mind, as he had hoped in the puzzle he had secreted away in his shoe.

Harry jumped in, 'Now we need to go back to St Mark's to read the full inscription on this Daphne's tombstone.'

'Yes, of course,' added Jim.

Kate, who was silent until now, chimed in, 'The trip to Muirford is necessary, of course, but all it will yield will be the date of Daphne's death and probably her age. But you need to do it. I suppose that's how detective work is done?'

'Yes, dear Kate,' said Jim, 'can't leave any clue unfinished. Besides, there must be something to the victim's elaborate scheme to hide this Daphne Welles's name and gravesite.'

The group broke up, Kate and Jim went out to Wilcote Hall and Milly and Harry back to the cottage.

The next day, Harry drove out to West Cornwall to find Daphne's tombstone. He was unlucky enough to arrive late afternoon when a storm was brewing and the light fading. He put on a coat and ventured into the churchyard. The wind had whipped up as the storm broke. The rain and lightning were doing their best to make this a repeat of Charles Fitzroy Keane's unhappy visit to this place. The tree branches swayed so wildly that Harry had to avoid walking under them for fear of one breaking off and doing him serious harm. He tried to wipe the rain from his face, treading warily as he struggled to find the grave. It was near to dark now and he needed a torch to read the weathered words on the gravestones.

When he did find the right one, sure enough, there was the inscription. Kate's clarity of thought had won out, but in addition to the date and age, there was the, "Daddy, I think I'll have a little sleep" epitaph. Harry made nothing of this but would let the others know just in case it was another elaborate cryptic message. This case was taking on all the hallmarks of an enigma within an enigma!

Just as he wondered why he bothered to make the trip at all, he felt a jolt and a sharp pain in his left arm. Someone had grabbed him from behind and plunged a knife into his upper arm. It was meant for his back, but the storm and wind and Harry's uneven steps had spoiled the stranger's aim. Harry turned rapidly and grabbed at his assailant. They wrestled for dear life and fell back onto one of the graves. Just as Harry reeled up to continue the struggle, the stranger was dead still, in fact dead! Harry had somehow managed to grab at the arm holding the knife, reverse its aim and direct it into the stranger's chest.

Harry was exhausted, sodden by the rain, and in shock, as he half-stumbled back to his car and drove the short distance to the Muirford police station. They covered him with a dry blanket. He was given a hot cup of cocoa, then stitched up and bandaged by a local doctor who was called to the station. Photos were taken of his wound and the knife. He wrote out a statement about the incident while a police car and wagon drove out to the cemetery to collect the dead stranger. Harry was sent to the local inn to get a good night's rest. He was to return to the police station the next morning to see the body and complete his report. He telephoned Milly lest she became alarmed by his not driving back to the cottage that night.

The whole business was wrapped up in an hour. The police sergeant had checked their files and identified the stranger as Finn Armitage, a local criminal who had a police record. The knife, photos, and report were sent to London and a week later, a police laboratory report stated that judging by the wounds to Keane and Harry, the knife was almost certainly the one that was used on

Keane. The police recovered fifty pounds from Armitage's jacket.

Harry returned two weeks later for the coronial enquiry which concluded that Armitage was almost certainly the person who stabbed Keane to death. Harry was exonerated when Armitage's death was adjudged as accidental due to the struggle. He was relieved. It was his first time in any form of armed combat, something all detectives are trained to expect, but few ever experience in the field. He had missed the war, but not his little skirmish at the cemetery. The shock would linger for some time.

While waiting for the coronial enquiry, Harry spent a week on leave at his bedsit where a new acquaintance from a room upstairs, Mrs Sarah Gately, offered to help with tidying up, shopping, laundry, and meals. He saw a local doctor to change the dressing on his arm and was almost his old self by the time he needed to front the coroner. He had called Milly to reassure her that his recovery was an easy one and Jim visited twice. Both were appraised about recent events at Muirford. Sarah Gately continued to check in on him every day and kept up the odd meal, laundering, and cleaning.

Milly insisted on Harry driving to the cottage on the weekend after the enquiry for more rest. Milly did a first-rate job of mothering and bossing her brother, while he slept, had meals, took short walks, and read the newspapers. Jim and Kate drove over on Sunday to check on the patient and stayed for lunch while they discussed the incident at St Mark's, and Harry's confirmation that Daphne Welles was sixteen years old when she died in March 1948. This was important news but by no means a clue about who she was and how she died. Harry would order a Scotland Yard search of obituaries and the death certificate to find out further details if they existed, which they feared not.

On the drive back to London, Harry and Jim juggled possibilities and questions. Was Daphne Welles Keane's daughter? On a wilder note, did Brogan-Moore have any connection with Daphne Welles or Charles Fitzroy Keane or both? Why did Keane and Welles have different surnames? A few days of enquiries yielded the news that Daphne Welles had died of consumption after spending two years at St Kevin's sanatorium in Cornwall, which would explain her burial at nearby St Mark's. Her parents had died a few years earlier of natural causes and there were no records of any other living relatives. The news that her parents had died — *both* parents — added another enigma to the growing collection. If her father had died years earlier, then who was Charles Fitzroy Keane?

'There goes our Charles, murderer, and MP theories, Jim,' said Harry in the bar at the Old Crown that evening. From having looked like the case was fast closing as having been solved, they were instead confronted by one obvious certainty — Finn Armitage, the local criminal that Harry had grappled with at St Mark's cemetery, was in the employ of the person who wanted Charles Fitzroy Keane killed. More puzzling was whether or not Daphne Welles was connected to Keane and in what way, and whether or not she was of any importance to Brogan-Moore MP. He and Jim even flipped it around to thinking that perhaps Keane had somehow been involved in Daphne Welles's death. Could she be Brogan-Moore's daughter or niece? The "roles" played by Keane and Brogan-Moore in this case were becoming blurred.

Harry and Jim wrote to the girls with the news they had uncovered so far and all their latest questions. Harry had the good sense to include in his note to Milly the simple and poignant sentence on Daphne's tombstone: *"Daddy, I think I'll have a little sleep."* Milly wrote back to organise a third meeting in Oxford, which was fast becoming a weekend jaunt for the group. Jim had also passed on the inscription in a note to his sister, Kate.

Once all four were together again at the Melrose Inn, drinks at hand and ready for Milly's reason for this gathering, Kate and Milly exchanged looks and knowing smiles. Kate couldn't help herself, 'So, you two are detectives!'

Harry and Jim looked at each other and at Kate self-consciously as Milly spoke,

'Didn't it occur to you two Scotland Yard sleuths that someone had ordered that inscription on the tombstone and that person would be Daphne's father?' Kate nodded in agreement as Milly added, 'Who do you think ordered the words on the tombstone: "Daddy, I think I'll have a little sleep?"'

Jim spoke for him and Harry, when he said, 'Look you two, detectives see clues every day and most, like this one for Daphne, go nowhere and are almost always diversions or conjectures. Of course, we considered that Keane might be her father but couldn't see how that is possible given the documented evidence about Welles's mother *and* father dying years earlier. Your feminine intuition is good as far as it goes. Of course, we still have the open question of whether Brogan-Moore was Daphne's father.'

Kate brought into this firmly and loudly in a way that took Harry and Jim aback, as she said,

'Intuition fiddlesticks. Daphne's father is Charles Fitzroy Keane. William Brogan-Moore is only a remote chance. Both of you have broached these possibilities and yet you two dunderheads dismissed out of hand any relevance to the case!'

Jim felt chastened by his own sister, her rebuke hurt his feelings *and* his ego, but he couldn't fail to notice that Kate was inculcating herself into this case with a passion that belied her previously soporific indifference.

Milly interjected, 'Okay, here's the plan of action. Kate and I will investigate Keane's past, while you two chase up our MP, which makes sense, as you will be in London and might be able to organise a meeting with him, but tread warily. We don't want to arouse too much suspicion at this stage. Lastly, we need to find out more about the mysterious Daphne Welles and this will require an official visit to the sanitorium. I don't think much will come of it, but we can't avoid it. It's not immediately urgent.' Harry said that he would make the trip after he and Jim had their meeting with Brogan-Moore.

The group did not disperse as usual because Jim had planned for all to meet the next day for lunch at Wilcote Hall. No one objected to this invitation, but Milly suspected that it might be so that she and Jim could spend more time together. There were no loose ends, new clues, or pressing matters that would suggest otherwise, and all their latest queries could wait until Monday.

Harry felt awkward, as Kate was as indifferent as ever, except for her latest blast, aided and abetted by his own sister! But he could not deny Jim the chance to romance Milly further, even if it was against her better judgement.

Harry's cottage it might have been, but the "deal" offered to the inspectors —by Milly — was that when Kate was in Oxford, they would have to take rooms at the Melrose Inn while Kate stayed at the cottage with Milly.

CHAPTER 5
William Brogan-Moore, MP

The now self-appointed "Oxford Four" arrived at the Hall on Sunday morning in glorious sunshine. Harry and Milly went to their usual rooms to freshen up. All four met downstairs and were whisked off to a side garden for morning tea. Richard, Helen, Dexter, and Lavinia were already present so that the expanded group of eight just managed to be seated at the large oval table, under a grand oak. There were rolling lawns and small flower beds in every direction and on one side, there was a single impressive rose garden. The group was shaded by the Hall and the large acorn oak. There was the usual banter around the table with two or three in separate conversations. Helen insisted on all staying for dinner. They could drive back early on Monday morning in time for work.

At dinner, all were attuned to talk about the case and all the latest clues and news. When mention was made of Brogan-Moore MP, Dexter offered a slight knowledge of him and his position in parliament. Richard didn't know Brogan-Moore but had heard about him from a friend in the House of Lords, whom Dexter also knew when reminded of the acquaintance by his father. Richard seemed almost to delight in this opportunity to inject a bit of mirth into the conversation with his House of Lords friend's recollection of Brogan-Moore as a pompous ass who affected an aristocratic air and a self-appointed reputation for oratory.

Richard retold his friend's story of a much earlier version of a "Brogan-Moore" type, 'There was, back in 1912, an MP who was full of bluster and considered himself one of life's great orators. Richard recalled Winston Churchill's erudite appraisal at the time, saying that the honourable member was, "one of those orators who before they get up, do not know what they are going to say, when they are speaking, do not know what they are saying, and when they have sat down, do not know what they have said."'

All laughed at this recollection. Dexter ventured to add that he had heard a couple of Brogan-Moore's speeches in the House.

'Anything like father's anecdote about Churchill's character reference for one such House "orator?"' asked Kate.

Dexter began, 'Well, let's put it this way, to say that Brogan-Moore's speeches are wooden would be an insult to wood.' Another round of laughter. He added, 'What do you expect from an ex-mathematician, now turned MP? But surely Brogan-Moore, a respected member of parliament, isn't one of your suspects?'

'Dexter,' Harry began, 'one of the first things we are taught at Scotland Yard is that "only Caesar's wife is above suspicion."' Jim nodded with an emphatic tilt of his head.

'And so should it be,' said Richard, as the party broke up and began to disperse to different parts of the Hall. Helen and Lavinia settled on the lounges, Richard went to his study to read and smoke a pipe, Dexter to practice billiards, leaving two couples to walk out onto separate side terraces.

Jim and Milly drifted out silently, turned to look at each other, and kissed in an embrace that was a romantic frisson if ever there was one. Jim was smiling at Milly, who couldn't help herself and was smitten by the evening moonlight, the idyllic location, the kiss, and the man holding her in his arms. Her resistance was over and what was to follow was ordained by the stars, at least so it seemed on this night. For the moment, she was in a fantasy land and didn't care, wanting it to last forever.

On the other terrace, a very different meeting was taking place. No chance of kisses here, even though the thought occurred fleetingly to Harry. Instead, Kate began as if this was an official briefing, and she was emboldened by their earlier knowing gazes that led to her words now.

'You and I know that we might be dealing with a very dangerous person in Brogan-Moore.' Harry nodded as she continued. 'He could have been at

Muirfold when the murder took place or organised it with that Armitage villain. That MP is arrogant and pompous and probably thinks he is above the law and can put it over, don't you think?'

'Yes, quite.' Harry's interjection was deliberately almost monosyllabic as he dare not interrupt Kate's stream of consciousness, which went on.

'Right, then you and Jim have a dangerous mission before you. We need to know how Brogan-Moore is involved in this case, so Milly and I will be depending on you two to bring us valuable news at our next meeting. Use all your resources at the Yard to dig up some dirt on him, if any exists.'

There was a pause as they concluded their "official" business, then Harry took a chance, in his awkward way, to be romantic, at least by word if not deed. He had to try something. This glacial beauty had him bewitched in this moonlit night, her elegance shining brighter than ever.

'Kate, have you read much Shakespeare or Byron?'

'That's an odd question. Why do you ask? Of course, I've read both poets.'

'Yes, I'm sure you have and indeed more than me, but I like to read verse from both when I have the time. I also crave any biographical details about their lives in the interesting periods in which they lived. Alas, most of that reading was many years ago. I sometimes recall Lord Byron's heroic travels through the Mediterranean, in Spain retracing the steps taken by the Moors, in

Greece and Italy, where empires grew and fell, in that most magnificent of cities, Venice, and across to Turkey and Asia. Did you know that Byron once swam the Hellespont, a distance of three miles, beginning in Europe and ending in Asia? And do you know that thereafter, typical of Byron, he cited it as his greatest achievement, placing it above his poetry?'

Kate was taken aback by this junior detective from humble origins, and no doubt little educated in her estimation, now sprouting about poets and history. Was he trying to impress her with his knowledge of the arts? She wasn't sure, but she had to say something.

'No, I didn't know that about Byron. I never read about his private life for fear of hearing more about what others have said of him. For instance, his libertine sojourn in Italy with the Shelleys, Keats, and others, and those horror stories about Dr Frankenstein. I always avoided these news items and chose instead to believe Lady Caroline Lamb's assessment of Byron as "mad, bad, and dangerous to know."'

Harry paused for a few seconds then was brazen enough to say, 'I'm sure there was a lot to say against Byron, and little for him, save for his poetry, but he once said something that I read and never forgot, which was, "always laugh when you can, it is cheap medicine". Don't you think that is wise counsel?'

Kate looked at him with a blank expression. No, she had never heard that advice but agreed that it was wise. She added,

'Byron was an English peer and poet but he strayed from the mainstream path of fame so that he is remembered as much for his misdeeds as for his poetry.'

Harry couldn't resist his next utterance, 'Then I expect you would not be enamoured of our famous, or is it infamous, Irish poet and writer, Oscar Wilde?'

'I confess he wrote well, but he was a rogue, like Byron,' she said, adding, 'You know, mixing their English and Irish origins doesn't make them any better, does it?'

'Oh, I don't know. Look at us, both with clashing first names, yours Irish and mine English.'

'Yes, Inspector Dillon, quite so. It's becoming quite cool out here; we should go inside.'

That was it for Harry. He had tried in his clunky way, without success, and wouldn't try again with such a cold fish of a girl, no matter how attractive! He made up his mind that this beauty was girdled in her hyphenated family name and had no time for trivialities and word games about names and poets. He decided that he was destined to miss all the loving in the world, at least in this neck of the world. He could see himself marrying a scullery maid or someone from across the Irish Sea at some time in the future.

Harry and Jim organised a meeting with Brogan-Moore in his office at noon on the Friday after the previous Oxford meeting and weekend at Wilcote Hall. William Brogan-Moore MP was of solid build, middle-aged, medium height, with a jutting chin.

'Come in, gentlemen, sit you down and tell me what I can do for the local constabulary.'

Jim began,

'Sir, we are investigating a murder at Muirford some weeks ago. A Mr Charles Fitzroy Keane of no fixed abode, of about forty-five years of age, was killed in his sleep at an inn at Muirford in West Cornwall. Earlier that evening he had visited a remote cemetery in a churchyard on a craggy bluff and during a raging storm. Would you have any idea, sir, of these events?'

'No, I've never been to that village, nor do I know anyone of that name, Detective Inspector Wilson-Smythe.'

Harry chipped in, 'Sir, if you do not know the deceased gentleman, could you tell us why you paid his burial expenses?'

Harry had set off his trap but was unprepared for Brogan-Moore's immediate reply, 'Yes, detective, no mystery there. I have a family friend, a vicar, who has a parish not far from Muirford. He called me when all this hullabaloo was going on and asked if I could help with the burial costs, as no one came forward to represent his family or offer to meet the funeral costs.'

Good answer, thought Harry who then tried a different angle. 'Family friend your vicar may be, Mr Brogan-Moore, but it still looks odd, doesn't it, that you covered the burial expenses of a complete stranger at the behest of this vicar? Why didn't the vicar simply ask for a pauper's burial, which the county would surely have given?'

'Right you are, inspector, but the vicar is well-acquainted with my role as an MP and he surmised, and I agreed, that news of this benevolence would assist my re-election later this year.'

It was Jim's turn to try to crack this MP's armour plating. 'If you were not acquainted with Mr Charles Fitzroy Keane, then, of course, you wouldn't know his daughter who is buried in St Mark's cemetery?'

'No, I didn't know that. What was her name?'

'That, sir, we do not yet know,' said Harry, fudging the truth to see if it got a rise out of the MP. It didn't, but Brogan-Moore stared at the wall behind the detectives as he turned over this response in his mind.

Then he asked the obvious question that Harry was expecting,

'If you don't know the daughter's name, Detective Inspector Dillon, how do you know she is buried in that cemetery?'

'Sir, at this stage of our investigation, that information is confidential. Look, we have taken up too much of your time, thank you for your cooperation,' said Harry as he sidled towards the door.

'Not at all, gentlemen, glad to help and I would be indebted to you if you would appraise me of any developments. I wouldn't want any adverse news to sully my benevolence in seeing to this man's burial costs.'

'Yes, sir, that we shall do,' said Harry, closing the door behind them.

'Well, what did you think of that performance, old man?' Jim flashed at Harry.

'Intriguing, but nothing to help us pin anything on him, yet. He is a cool customer and will be hard to break down, if indeed he is guilty as we suspect.' He added, 'I wonder what the girls would make of Mr Brogan-Moore?'

'More than we did, I am sure, given their voracious propensity to intuit almost everything in this case! Let's get a drink then call them to another meeting at our Oxford inn, weekend after this one, eh, Harry.'

'Ah no, can't drink now, sorry, Jim, I am booked to see a new film with a woman who boards in my building. She is a bit of a film buff, so I'm going on her recommendation. See you on Monday,' said Harry, as he shook hands with his friend then paced quickly down the street.

Harry freshened up back in his bedsit, then went up the stairs to the unit above and knocked on the door. 'Are you in, Mrs Gately?'

'Yes, Harry, come in, the door is open.' Sarah Gately, whose help Harry had enjoyed during his convalescence, was slim, very attractive, and a war widow, with no children, and about forty years of age and lived alone.

'We've met too often now for you to keep calling me *Mrs* Gately — it makes me feel so old, especially now that I've reached the dreaded age of... never mind the age... just call me Sarah, or just plain "Gately," as you young people seem to have a hankering to do these days with names!'

'Sarah it is then. By the way, which film are we seeing?'

'It's new, filmed last year in bombed-out Vienna in Austria. If you were a film buff, you'd know the stars, producers, and director as I do, which is why I expect it to be very, very good. I've read one review in *The Times* and it was glowing in suggesting that it would become a cinema classic. It's black and white *film noir* — shadowy and dark, creepy, full of suspicious looking characters, twists, mystery, murder, a reputedly wonderful musical score, oh, and a bumbling investigating officer, right up your alley,' she said smiling at that reference to the officer.

'Thank you, Sarah for the character reference,' he said, smiling back at his friend. 'By the way, you haven't told me the name of the film?'

'Oh, sorry, it's called *The Third Man*, and it has a big star in it, Orson Welles, who is famous for the absolute classic *Citizen Kane*, that he made in 1941.'

'Never heard of him or his film.' He had paused to reflect for a moment on the name 'Welles' but dismissed it as a simple coincidence. After all, it is a fairly common name.

'You will hear of him, Harry,' she said, in what would be a prophetic statement.

So, off to the flicks they went and thoroughly enjoyed the film. On the walk back to their bedsits, both agreed that it was indeed a brilliant film, destined for high honour. Harry thought to himself that he should see Orson Welles and his *Citizen Kane* if he could find it showing somewhere in perhaps a film retrospective. He mentioned this to Sarah and she offered to keep watch for it.

A small bud took shape in Harry's mind as he walked back down the stairs to his room. Sarah was quite a bit older than him, but she was very bright and still very attractive with no children or other diversions. Maybe he could try romance on her? He would think about it in the coming days, but it was tempting. She is always kind and pleasant, easy-going, and very good company, well-read and educated. "Sarah Dillon" sounds all right, and not a hyphen in sight! Being brave and forward with girls had always been a bugbear, but on a scale of climbing Mount Everest, he could meet Sarah about mid-climb, but with Kate, he was stuck in the base camp!

The next chance that Harry had to talk with Sarah was about a week later when they had arranged to meet up for morning tea in a quaint little café on the corner of the block they lived in. Harry looked across the table at his attractive companion, but he didn't want to look aggressive or pressing in his questions. He led off with,

'Tell me, Sarah, I know your life is fairly full, what with movies, reading and collecting books, and going out and about to some show or exhibition.'

'Yes, now that you put it that way, I suppose it is, but I've always time for friends like you, Harry.'

'Thank you, Sarah, you are very kind, but that wasn't what I was getting at. Look, I hope you don't take this the wrong way, but you are a very attractive woman, and since you have no family to occupy your time and affections, have you ever considered finding a man to walk out with now and then?'

'How very quaintly you put that, Harry, and thank you for the compliment. Believe me, at my age, having a younger man say such a thing is very heartening. I'll cherish your remark. Now about "walking out with someone", goodness do people still use such an expression?'

'Probably not, I read it in an old book and liked its cuteness.'

'Well, as it happens, I am walking out with someone, but I cannot advertise it as it would be construed as illegal.'

'Oh, I don't understand, Sarah, is the man wanted by the law?'

'No, and it's not a man, it's a woman, and I am the one who would be wanted by the law!'

Harry's mouth was slightly agape as she continued, 'She is about my age and we like the same things. I've had her over a few times and vice versa. You know I recognised a tendency to like other girls back in high school, but we were taught to avoid such things and very little ever happened. So, I played the normal game of marrying a good man from a good family. Before we could start a family, war broke out and he was killed. But these past few years have rekindled my adolescent urges. My new friend and I are very attracted to one another and a few tender kisses have passed between us so far. We treasure each other's company. If it lasts, who knows what might happen? There, I've confessed. Knowing this now, Inspector Dillon, are you going to arrest me?'

'Of course not, Sarah. I've read about this stuff and I know what the law says. There was that infamous Oscar Wilde trial at which he was accused of being a sodomite. Why do we torture genius, or even ordinary people, for having different feelings? I've never forgotten one utterance which occurred at his trial. The prosecutor asked him about his wanderings around London, with one area in particular mentioned. Wilde was asked if that neighbourhood was disreputable, and he replied unblinkingly, "Yes, disreputable for sure, I believe it is very near the Houses of Parliament." Even then, under cross-examination, with a long gaol sentence ahead, his humour flourished.'

Sarah chuckled as Harry continued, 'Besides, you only need to look at the Bible, great book, but the Old Testament is full of sensational stuff. Brother murdering brother, Sodom and Gomorrah and its so-called perversions. You know the only story of goodness that I ever remembered out of that book was Solomon's wise counsel when two women came before him disputing who was the rightful mother of a newborn baby. They even taught that one to us in detective school. King Solomon had wisdom for sure, and they say you only become wise as you age.'

Sarah came in, 'Harry, you don't need to be old to be wise, and as I've found, you don't even need to be religious. It might sound trite, but all you need is to be able to distinguish right and wrong. That's the answer to all those Bible conundrums about slaying brothers, jealousy, rage, avarice and so on.'

Harry asked, 'So where does wisdom fit in all of this?'

'I'm glad you asked. When I was much younger, maybe fifteen or so, I was suffering all that teenage angst fuelled by hormones and seeing all the world as against me. In those times, parents were private enemy number one! Anyway, one day my father took me aside and told me a story that must have been a parable from the Bible. His hope was that I would see wisdom in the old man in this tale. There was an elderly man who owned a large tract of land which he farmed and ran goats and sheep. His two sons helped him, and he made them work and work. One day he said to his sons, "I am going to divide my land into two sections and each of you will take one as his own. That way, there will be no disputes when I am gone."'

'Over the next few days, the father divided the land roughly in half but as it had an irregular perimeter, he couldn't be sure that the halves were equal. One of his sons came to him and said that he was worried that his brother would get the bigger plot. The father looked at him, "My son, I love you both the same and I've tried to divide the land into equal halves. Your brother told me that he is happy with the way I've done this. But if you are not pleased, *you* choose the block you want and your brother will take the other."'

'Simple but wise, eh, Harry.'

'I wish that life's problems could all be that simple,' said Harry.

'Life's too short to be simple, Harry. We need problems to solve, people to love, or mourn over, jobs to do, wars to fight.'

'Why, Sarah, you are a born philosopher!'

'No, I'm not, but there is something in saying that "life is too short". We live in a passing parade of time with connections to the past and future generations in our little window of life. People are like plants, with old roots in the ground and new shoots reaching for sunlight. The roots are our past, rigid, and set but directing how the plant will grow. The green shoots, stems, and small branches are the new members of the family. It's why we refer to them as "family trees." The more twigs and branches, the more remote family members become, but the plant is still the giver of life and different branches overlap and wither or grow as time moves on.'

Sarah was warmed up now and was speaking at and beyond Harry, as she continued, 'We know and remember grandparents, parents, siblings, children, grandchildren, and those mostly of our generation and those on either side. Oh, of course, there are history books, photos, stories spun by elders, mementoes from parents, remembrances of childhood and so on. But the next generation to ours loses all contact with one section of their past, and they inherit a whole new group of people into their world. That's why the lessons and stories of the past are so important, the future beyond our own lives far less so. You know, I have a few very nice pink cake plates left to me by my grandmother. It's not much, we weren't well-to-do, but every time I use those plates, I think of her. That's one of my contacts with the past and soon, even that will be gone.' Tears welled in her eyes.

Harry waded in to try to cheer her up, 'You *are* a born philosopher, and a first-rate one at that!'

Sarah giggled, wiped the tears, and said, 'Now back to me and my situation. What are you to do with your promiscuous friend?'

'Damn! Didn't bring handcuffs with me today, but I know where you live.' They both smiled as he added, 'I think this wisdom stuff is starting to rub off on me, Sarah. I look at you and all I see is love. Besides, my job doesn't cover making judgements about people like you and your friend. I haven't witnessed you breaking any law, and nor do I expect to. You're a good egg, Sarah, and the best of friends.'

They both rose to leave, and she came over to him, leant across to hug and kiss him warmly on the cheek and knew that he too was a good egg!

As they walked back to their bedsit, Sarah asked how the case was coming along. Harry said that they had dug up a few clues, but you know how slowly these things go. He told her about the odd puzzle on the scrap of paper, and the name of the victim, and that his daughter might be buried in that cemetery, but there was the problem of different surnames, the girl buried at St Mark's was called Daphne Welles. He told Sarah how it seemed an odd coincidence that here they had just seen Orson Welles in *The Third Man* and there was Daphne Welles in that graveyard. Just as he finished telling Sarah this news, she grabbed his arm, sat them both down on a bus bench and gave him her "solution" to the disguises adopted by, or given to, father and daughter. Harry was amazed at Sarah's cleverness and told her that he couldn't wait to tell the others at their next Oxford meeting.

When he and Sarah reached home, Harry closed the door behind him, sat down and stared at the blank wall in front of him and said to himself, "Oh well, bad luck, old man, no future with that attractive woman, but I'm happy for her and pleased that she has companionship. Loneliness must be one of the saddest things in this world. Maybe it's the price we pay for growing old. Or is it just down to luck, depending on when and where you are born, if you have family or friends, who dies, who lives, which window of time you live in?"

Harry recalled the old proverb about *only the good dying young*, and his near miss in almost ending up "good, young, and *dead*" back at St Mark's. He hoped that that would be his only brush with death. He would be happier growing old but not alone. He needed a romantic partner. The urge was there but he would worry about it later. Presently, he had his first serious case to solve; and he had a very, very interesting story to tell his friends and sister at the next Oxford get-together.

CHAPTER 6
Charles Fitzroy Keane

A meeting of the "Oxford Four" was called for the following Saturday at the Melrose Inn. Harry and Jim had driven up together. Kate came up on the Friday evening and spent the night at the cottage with Milly. As the group assembled for lunch, Harry noticed a change in Milly's demeanour. She was looking sullen this day and not her usual excited self. He figured that she was a little exasperated by their lack of progress. And Kate, Kate was Kate. Beautiful and remote as always, with that patrician air. Yes, base camp at Everest was as far as he was likely to go with this young beauty.

During their casual banter before getting down to serious business, Harry ventured the news that he had seen an excellent film the other day.

'I'm not really a film person, but this was brilliant — dark, intriguing, mysterious, great music, and with excellent actors. It's called *The Third Man*.'

'Oh, yes, I've read a review about it and was planning to see it soon,' offered Kate. 'I do so like noirish and gothic books and films.'

Harry went on, 'So you should, Kate. I can see you enjoying its sullen moodiness. The actress in it even looks a bit like you, perhaps a little prettier.' His gander was up and for once he was enjoying himself throwing a dart towards Kate's "statue of beauty" — he had deleted "statuesque beauty" some time ago.

Kate's eyes fixed him with a wry smile.

'Harry, how insulting, how can you speak to Kate like that?' chided Milly.

Jim laughed, 'Milly, he is pulling your leg, our legs, just a joke to see if he can penetrate Kate's steely poise, right, Kate?'

'Yes,' was Kate's reply, delivered between clenched teeth.

'Anyway, what I didn't mention was that it was my neighbour in the flat upstairs, Sarah Gately, who took me to the film.'

'Oh, you've never mentioned her before,' said Milly.

'Didn't need to until now, sis. She's a war widow, forty, no children, and very attractive.'

'Oh,' pushed Kate, 'is *she* prettier than the girl in the film?'

'Right, then, on to business,' interjected Jim quickly, before Kate motioned to empty her drink into Harry's lap! He needn't have worried; Harry simply smiled. She had got him back nicely. At least she can take a joke and has a sense of humour.

Harry went on with his news about *The Third Man*. 'Did you know that one of the stars of that film is Orson Welles?' No one nodded, so he continued, 'Do you note that name "Welles?"'

Milly spoke up, 'Come on, Harry, how does a girl's name that's been on a tombstone for what, two years, have anything to do with an actor in a film that's just been released?'

'I'll tell you, and it's a very clever story, but I will not claim the glory for myself. After the movie, Sarah my film buff neighbour and I retired to a café for tea and cake and on the way home, I told her about our victim and Daphne Welles, the disguised name in our puzzle. Sarah was very helpful in coming forth with some valuable information about our case.'

'Really, Harry, now you are stretching credulity. What the dickens could she figure from a couple of names?' Milly again.

Harry then launched into Sarah's encyclopaedic knowledge of films. 'Do any of you know that Orson Welles was the director and star of the 1941 film *Citizen Kane*? Apparently, it's something of a classic and very controversial when it was released. The studio came under a lot of pressure to suppress the film.'

Only Kate had a vague recollection of it, as she said, 'Now 1941 is what, seven or eight years before Daphne was interred at St Mark's, right? So, what's the significance between Mr Welles and Daphne Welles?'

'Go on,' said Jim to Harry, wanting him to finish his news.

'Our murder victim wanted to disguise himself and Daphne's gravesite. What if he was a film fan, and on a whim, took an interest in *Citizen Kane* and Mr Welles as a device to hide themselves from pursuers?' Now that he had warmed up, the others were listening intently.

'That is what Sarah thinks, that Welles is not Daphne's real name. What if Charles Fitzroy Keane gave her that name? Nor is Keane a real name. Are you ready for the next little gem? In *Citizen Kane*, Orson Welles's character has the name Charles Foster Kane. Does that tell you anything?'

Kate broke in, 'Charles Fitzroy Keane *is* a false name, and it's a disguise matched from Charles Foster Kane, CFK! So, Daphne could indeed have been given Welles's name.'

'You've got it, Kate,' exclaimed Harry, as Milly and Jim nodded in agreement with these comparisons. 'But that's not all, we also need to note that CFK and Daphne have different last names.'

'So, they are not father and daughter?' asked Jim.

'That bit is still vague. They might not be, or they could be. Don't forget, the father's inscription on Daphne's tomb, "Daddy, I think I'll have a little sleep," as you two girls insisted previously. Sarah figured that CFK wanted to leave more than one distracting clue and so called his daughter "Welles," instead of "Keane." It would be more difficult to trace two different bogus names.'

'Could be,' thought Milly out loud.

Harry continued, 'My friends, now comes yet another connection with *Citizen Kane*. According to Sarah, in the film, there is a grand gothic castle that Charles Foster Kane, now a rich press baron, built for himself, and he named the castle *Xanadu*, after the mythical grand palace of the Mongol conqueror Kubla Khan, as told in Samuel Taylor Coleridge's poem of that name.'

Milly interrupted, 'Very nice literature lesson, Harry, but how does that help us with this case?'

'I'll tell you, sis. Sarah mentioned that the film *Citizen Kane* was a thinly veiled jab at an American publishing tycoon, William Randolph Hearst, who built his own pleasure palace on a coastal bluff in California, and called it *San Simeon*, which Welles conveniently swapped for *Xanadu* in his film. It was Hearst, using all his press baron powers, who tried to have the film withdrawn and all copies destroyed.'

Harry enjoyed seeing his audience now waiting on every word. 'The next bit was all my doing, Milly, and I was pleased that we didn't need your cryptographer this time! If you rearrange the letters of Hearst's *San Simeon* into a single word, you come up with 'Massinone,' the non-existent town where our Charles Fitzroy Keane lived. That makes three connections with *Citizen Kane*! CFK, Daphne Welles, and Massinone, all of which CFK must have cleverly adopted, probably in fear of Brogan-Moore finding them out.'

'Nice work, Harry,' conceded Milly, with Jim and Kate agreeing. She continued, 'Hang on, that's all very well parcelled up, but it couldn't have been a very good disguise because CFK's killer knew where to find him, tracked him down, and killed him in his sleep.'

Harry had to admit, 'Blast, yes, Milly, that is a sticking point. But it doesn't change the use of the three disguised names, does it?'

'No, it doesn't, Harry,' said Kate, joining in. 'There's a missing thread here, MPs have ways of ordering all sorts of searches. If Brogan-Moore was somehow able to trace Daphne Welles to the sanitorium, he could have pored over the visitor's book and found that her only visitor was CFK. Or Brogan-Moore could have arranged for a crony to stake out the place and discover that CFK was the only visitor. And that crony could be the person who killed CFK, and later attacked you, Harry.'

Jim almost yelled, 'So are we still in the hunt?'

Milly answered, 'Yes, we are, Jim, but we still need to connect Brogan-Moore directly to CFK and Daphne, and to discover how he found CFK, first at St Kevin's sanatorium, then in his room at Muirford, don't we? That's the missing thread Kate mentioned.'

'Yes, sis, that's the gist of it, but we will get there if we keep digging.'

They agreed to leave it there for now and work on it during the coming days. Milly and Jim walked out of the tavern together in deep discussion, then Kate and Harry moved out to the street, behind them but in silence. Milly and Jim had joined hands and were embracing off to one side and mostly out of view of the other two. There was a refreshing breeze that rustled the leaves of the nearby trees. There were far more bicycles than cars on the road, but being Oxford, that was more usual than not, with students everywhere.

Then something happened that took Harry completely off-guard. Kate turned to him and asked,

'Why haven't you ever tried to kiss me?'

Tongue-tied and speechless, Harry gulped and gathered a reply, 'Actually, to be honest, I did think of it, but baulked... er... for two reasons. Firstly, you've been so cool that I didn't think you had any interest in me. Secondly, if I were brazen enough to attempt it, I'm sure a well-timed slap to the face would end that little adventure!'

Kate looked at Harry, whose face was still puzzled by her inquisition, albeit a pleasant one, he told himself. Suddenly, she moved across the gap between them and kissed him lightly, put his arm around her waist, drew him in, then kissed him passionately.

He spoke, bravely for once, 'You know, I could get used to this.'

'So could I,' came the reply, as she moved in and kissed him again.

Then Harry took pause to ask, 'But aren't you betrothed to some rich and aristocratic landowner or cousin, once, twice, or thrice-removed?'

'Yes, I am, cousin, once-removed, in fact, but what of it?'

Harry thought about this carefully as he stared blankly at Kate's very pretty face. Is this just a side fling for her while she awaits her gentrified future? Is she looking for a trifling dalliance to while away life's boredom? He didn't care, and why would he with this rare chance to embrace this very beautiful young woman? He was even sanguine in his own complicity, telling himself that this would be good practice for when he would meet a new girlfriend. After a pause, while he mulled over these thoughts, he said, 'Nothing really,' was his simple reply. He *was* being devious, but hang it, it was she who was cheating on her fiancé, not him.

She added, 'Then let's make it even more memorable,' as she moved in and kissed him again and again.

'I'm not a complete fool, Kate, I know you are using me, like one of those rag dolls that becomes so frayed that it is thrown out with the rubbish. But I'll play along until your cousin turns up.'

'Good man.'

Meanwhile, Jim and Milly had finished their own kissing interlude and re-joined the other two who had by now disengaged.

And so ended the last of the "Oxford Four" meetings at the Melrose Inn, for reasons good and ill that would soon become clear.

CHAPTER 7
Engagement

In Xanadu did Kubla Khan a stately pleasure-dome decree... begins Samuel Taylor Coleridge's romantic poem. Randolph Hearst's *San Simeon* was real enough, but *Xanadu and* Massinone, alas, were not.

A long car trip brought Harry to St Kevin's sanitorium near Muirford, where Daphne Welles was treated for consumption before she died. Along the way, Harry daydreamt of his recent pleasant interlude with Kate. Would it happen again? Of course not, so he put it out of his mind — for good he hoped — just as he arrived at the sanitorium.

At the reception desk, he produced his Scotland Yard ID card and then settled down on a lounge to scan through the reception and record books that were brought to him. Sure enough, there were multiple entries for Charles Fitzroy Keane over the two years of Daphne's illness. A copy of the death certificate was produced and in it were the already-known particulars of Daphne's cause and date of death. The certificate was signed by a Dr J Leland. When Harry asked if Dr Leland was their usual doctor, the answer came that they really didn't have one and they contact whoever is either on their books, in the town, or recommended by another doctor who is too busy to attend. Harry drove back to London and passed on the information in notes sent to Milly and Kate, and verbally to Jim at their next Old Crown lunch.

A week passed without event or progress, possibly because plans were well afoot for an imminent engagement party at Wilcote Hall. The happy couple had been seeing each other often and their romance gathered strength until Richard and Helen Wilson-Smythe sent out invitations for an engagement party to be held at the Hall on the 14 September 1950 in the early afternoon. Harry had already celebrated with them separately, first at the Old Crown with Jim, then with Milly one weekend at Oxford. He couldn't help but notice how both had beamed with joy, perhaps Milly more so, in seeing this aristocratic family take her into their arms.

Certainly, Helen, Kate, and Lavinia were very amiable, and fussed over her during recent guest visits to the Hall. Kate insisted on taking Milly to her dressmaker in London to commission a frock befitting the happy event. Kate had become very fond of Milly. Harry noticed her attention and he was grateful to her for making his sister so welcome. Apparently, Kate's "temperature" rose and fell with whatever fancy took her and with whomever she was with, or so Jim confided to his friend.

On went the arrangements, until finally the day arrived, and all forty guests and family gathered on the main lawn for the festivities. Bright sunlight and only a zephyr of a breeze provided the guests with the best possible weather.

A brief introduction and short speech by Richard was followed by an abundance of food, drink, and happy milling around the tables and gardens.

A tap on the shoulder caused Harry to turn around and there stood Dexter with a stranger who was introduced as Dr J Leland. A shock went up Harry's spine, but he tried very hard to disguise it. He had only uncovered Dr Leland's role in Daphne's death at St Kevin's not two weeks ago! After a few pleasantries about the weather and the party, Harry excused himself and moved over to Kate, motioning with a tilt of his head to walk to an oak tree just to the side of the main group of guests.

He pointed the doctor out and told her his name. She was expressionless with puzzlement, as he said, 'But Kate, he must be a family friend?'

'Never set eyes on him before today,' came her answer.

'I count what, twenty or so people here who are not family and Dr Leland happens to be one of them! Are you fobbing me off about this doctor and his connection with your family?'

'No, of course not. It's the first time I've ever seen him. Look, let's leave it for now lest we upset Jim and Milly. We can talk about it tomorrow.'

'We'll see,' said Harry suspiciously.

Of course, he believed her, why should she lie? Or was he so taken in by her untouchable beauty that he'd believe anything she would say? The two split up and moved about the crowd, engaging here and there with family and other guests. Then Jim rushed over to Harry, grabbed his arm, and motioned to the stairs descending from a side terrace onto the lawn. A late guest had arrived. Lo, it was the unmistakable person of William Brogan-Moore MP.

Milly and then Kate doubled this little group, and the girls were made aware of the new guest's name. Odd looks all round. Then Kate bit her tongue and indicated to Milly and Jim the presence of the other surprise guest, Dr J Leland, standing just off to the left under an elm tree. Harry looked at his sister and Jim, and said,

'I'm sorry, you two, but it looks like we've spoiled your party. Who would credit these two people turning up here today?'

'Harry, you haven't spoiled anything,' Jim injected, 'this case has brought Milly and me together, but it's still an unsolved murder and,' looking at Milly who nodded approvingly, 'we, all of us, will be more determined to solve it.'

By now, Harry was at least relieved to know that Kate had never laid eyes on these two mystery guests before today and he and Jim had only met Brogan-Moore that one time in his office at Parliament House a couple of weeks ago. Yet, there was no denying the oddity of both of these men just happening to turn up at the Hall this day for an invitation-only party. All four were thoroughly perplexed and would give all their attention to trying to figure out what was going on.

The remainder of the weekend was uneventful and as happy as it could be, after the shock of seeing those two unexpected guests. The now "Wilcote Four" decided against discussing the surprise party guests for fear of upsetting Jim's parents. They determined that they would carry out investigations elsewhere, and if there were no successes, then they could put it in the lap of the family at Wilcote in a week or so.

Jim and Harry returned to London and Milly to Oxford. Kate went down to London mid-week and asked Harry to lunch, a surprise invitation but one that was not to be refused, even on pain of being dismissed from the force for dereliction of duty in being out of the office without permission. He told himself that he was immune to her effect on him, then countered that thought by admitting to himself that he was well and truly hooked, even if she was engaged to her cousin, once removed. He resigned himself to this young woman merely toying with him in her spare time, but he was smitten enough to be unable to steel himself against her attentions. She could ask him almost anything and he would find it difficult to refuse, and most worrying, he suspected that she knew it! Was he too easy for her to manipulate to her whims? A rhetorical question for sure.

They met for lunch on Wednesday at a small café not far from Scotland Yard. Kate was friendly enough but not as effusively so as she had been that last time at Oxford. It turned out that she had an ulterior motive for this London visit and it involved Harry only as go-between.

'Harry, I would like to meet your friend Mrs Sarah Gately to learn more about this *Citizen Kane* film.'

'Why, do you think there is anything in it other than CFK's clever disguises for himself and his daughter?'

'Yes, I do, and I'll tell you at dinner tonight if you can rustle up afternoon tea with your attractive friend, Sarah.' The "dinner tonight" he suspected was a reward for him for setting up a meeting with Sarah. He had no intention of refusing either request. The meeting with Sarah was about his murder investigation that could yield another clue and the evening dinner with Kate he was happy to accept as another chance to try to work her out.

Harry and Kate were greeted warmly by Sarah as they moved into the front parlour where tea and cake were already set. Kate was taken aback a little in now realising that Harry wasn't pretending about Sarah to make her jealous. She was indeed very attractive, not looking her age, despite being informally dressed and without makeup! Were she not obviously older than

Harry, she could see them teaming up, which, of course, was the very thought that possessed Harry for a short time until he found out that Sarah was already spoken for, as they say.

They sat down to tea, and after the usual introductions and pleasantries, Harry began,

'Sarah, as you know, I have this very odd murder to solve and it is proving to be a difficult one. Mind you, it's my first, so of course, it is difficult. You know how Milly, Jim, and Kate here are putting our heads together on it. We've made progress, especially with your help from the *Citizen Kane* clues, but we are becalmed looking for more clues. Kate wanted to meet you as she thinks that there might be more to this *Citizen Kane* angle, but I confess to seeing it only being used for cryptic disguises by our victim.'

Sarah kept nodding agreeably when Kate loomed with, 'Mrs Gately.'

'Sarah, please call me Sarah.'

'Very well, Sarah, unlike my brother and Harry here, I suspect even more sinister intentions in this case and especially now that we have two players in William Brogan-Moore MP and a Dr J Leland.'

'Interesting,' Sarah began, 'I think I've seen your MP's name in *The Times* over some government piffle or other. But this is the first I've heard of a Dr J Leland. Harry, may I ask if you know Dr Leland's first name?'

'We don't, Sarah. Dr J Leland is how it appeared on Daphne's death certificate and in the register at St

Kevin's sanitorium. He turned up at Milly and Jim's engagement, and being a doctor, meant that everyone simply addressed him as "doctor" or "Dr Leland." His first name was never mentioned. You know how these titled persons are addressed. Even if his first name was known, most people would still address him as "Doctor."'

'Quite so,' said Kate.

'Well,' said Sarah, 'I can tell you that there is no doubt that your Charles Fitzroy Keane and Dr J Leland knew one another.'

'What?' exclaimed Kate, before Harry could utter the same word. Both now stared at Sarah expectantly.

'In *Citizen Kane*, Charles Foster Kane's best friend was Jedidiah Leland; but he wasn't a doctor.

Harry got in first with, 'But that's crazy!'

'No, it's not,' said Kate instantly. 'Yes, they were known to one another, probably old school friends or cousins or whatnot, but it's clear that Dr Leland attended Daphne's death and arranged her burial, but there is more to it than just that. While I'm sure that Leland, as a doctor, would not arouse any suspicion at St Kevin's sanitorium, more puzzling is the fact that CFK gave himself and Daphne Welles their fake names some time earlier, just as CFK must have asked his friend to take Leland's name for his sanitorium visits. But why did the doctor need a name disguise?'

Kate paused, stumped by her own question, and this gave Sarah and Harry the opportunity to jump in with their own observations.

'This is very frightening,' said Sarah, adding, 'CFK took precautions in the three name disguises, his hometown of Massinone, *and* the puzzle he left to be found by the police. He must have been worried that Brogan-Moore would find Daphne's gravesite, or Dr Leland, or CFK himself, but only CFK was the unlucky one in meeting his killer on that devilish night at Muirford.'

'Right you are, Sarah, but something else just occurred to me,' Harry said, 'Brogan-Moore and Dr Leland were *both* at Wilcote Hall the other day but it looks like neither was aware of the other's presence or was that a ruse by both of them? Maybe they know one another after all? I confess that this is rather perplexing.'

'Yes,' threw in Kate, 'but have you two not wondered why Dr Leland was at Wilcote Hall in the first place? Oh, we could possibly explain away Brogan-Moore as a friend of Dexter's, which we can wheedle out of him later, but not Leland. My family talked about him at dinner mid-week after the party and no one had ever heard of him. Can you beat that? Somehow, he had inveigled his way into the party, probably with a fake invitation. But why turn up, what was his purpose?

Harry then spoke. 'Milly and I also talked about Leland and could only take a wild guess that he somehow knows one or both of your parents, Kate, or is another of Dexter's odd friends from his club in London? His connection with CFK and Daphne can't be purely a circumstantial coincidence of Daphne's death at the sanitorium, and we still have Brogan-Moore to fit into this mess somehow?'

Sarah chipped in, 'Coincidences abound, of course, but not this time. The three name disguises of *Citizen Kane* origin are too strong to ignore.'

Harry said that he and Jim would get onto investigating Dr Leland this coming week back at the Yard. If nothing came of it, they could check with Jim's parents and Dexter the following weekend. He and Kate rose and thanked Sarah for her film buff talent and contributions. Harry drove Kate to her hotel, then made his way back to his humble digs in the flat below Sarah at the bedsit in Edgeware Road. He scrambled to find enough money — borrowing from Sarah as well — to pay for dinner that evening with Kate at the Savoy, her choice, of course. Harry couldn't resist asking Sarah what she thought of Kate.

'Beautiful, clever, snappy dresser, rich, and very attracted to you, dear friend.'

'No, no, no, wrong on the last one, Sarah, she is to marry a cousin, once removed.'

'I once removed a cousin — from my will! And I have no doubt that she will remove hers in due course, from her future.'

Harry chuckled at Sarah's *bon mot* about her will, then said, 'Sarah, people like Kate and her family live by tradition and the first law of tradition is to marry among the gentry and family to keep money and property out of reach of the hoi polloi.'

'Call it a woman's intuition if you like, but I saw the way she kept looking across at you. She's smitten, my boy, but doesn't want to admit it or drop her guard. You're still young, but a word of advice, all women want to be romanced, from whichever class they belong. The haughtier ones look cool and mannered, that's the main difference. They are raised to look and feel superior, never timid, or shy. You're just not used to women like that. Tell you what, you've borrowed five pounds towards this dinner tonight. If I'm wrong, you pay back the loan, but if I'm right, we are square.'

'Whatever you say, Sarah, but I'll put away a fiver from next payday, because I'm sure I'll need to repay it.'

Harry washed and dressed in his best clobber and ventured on to the Savoy. He reached the restaurant dining room fifteen minutes early; his eagerness was tempered by being savvy enough to know not to keep a girl waiting. From his vantage point at the pre-booked table, he watched as Kate entered the room and swept across the floor in an evening dress that emphasised her figure.

He was smitten all right and had to swallow to clear his throat to greet his dinner companion as he rose to help her into her chair. She asked him why he was staring at her so oddly and his easy reply was, 'Because you look even more beautiful than usual.'

'Piffle! An expensive evening frock, hair made up, and rouge on cheeks. You have a very pretty sister. Haven't you seen her in the plain light of day, and then dressed up at night for a ball or dinner?'

'Yes, of course, right you are. But I can't help noticing that, in your case, the transition has been from beauty to goddess.'

'Dear Harry, you are sweet. Such compliments should be rewarded, so don't forget the pledge I give you now. Should my cousin fall at the first hurdle, your name will be the next in my little book. After this evening, you will be known as my "cousin, twice removed."'

'Now you're mocking me. There'll be no more compliments from me this evening.' Milly had once told him that he had a great smile, so he affected it as best he could as Kate motioned for the waiter and ordered drinks.

'Two G&Ts please.'

'Yes, madam, right away.'

The rest of the evening was spent enjoying a first-rate meal, going through each other's family trees, touching briefly on the case but deciding it was best left for now, smiling at each other, making silly little jokes, and generally enjoying each other's company. Harry was bold enough to ask about Kate's cousin. What was his name, how often did they meet, and when was the wedding to be held? She fielded his questions with almost monosyllabic answers: Ralph Curtis-Higgins, not often, not sure. Harry looked glum despite Kate's indifferent second and third answers. Here was another hyphenated aristocrat! Harry called for the bill but was told by the waiter, discreetly, that madam had already charged it to her room. This annoyed him and he told Kate so, adding how demeaning it was for him to be treated as a poor companion.

'Cousin, twice removed, you are next in line if my cousin, once removed stands me up at the altar, so you need to save all your money.' She was enjoying being facetious and half-mocking, thinking that her paying the bill was not in any way demeaning. 'After all, Harry, it was my invitation, not yours. So, it becomes a matter of protocol.'

'Very funny, Kate, have your little jokes at my expense, I'm not without pride, you know.'

'Dignity suits you better. Besides, Milly told me how you would react.'

'My own sister conspiring with you against me! Wait until I see her again.'

'You will do no such thing, why she is practically family now, and we wouldn't want you going round insulting the Wilson-Smythes.' She was indeed enjoying throwing these barbs. He was on her patch tonight and an easy target.

They moved out into the foyer where Harry, now quite annoyed, gave Kate a curt,

'Goodbye, I hope you enjoy the rest of your evening.'

She arched one eyebrow towards him and said, 'Just when I was going to invite you up to my room.'

'Great, great, one indignity heaped on another. Here in London, away from your cousin, you want to drag me into a fling to ease your boredom.' Before he could take his next breadth, Kate delivered a very well-placed slap to his face. He put his hand to his reddened cheek, turned and left, treading heavily on the carpet, and racing down the stairs out into the bitterly cold evening. What Harry did not see was Kate, tears welling in her eyes, moving on to her room.

This had not gone well for either of them. Perhaps the impossibility of it all had caught them up in webs of their own making? Whatever it was, this was their very first tiff, and they weren't even engaged, let alone married! Harry tried to console himself by thinking that this is how spoilt girls behave, taking up dalliances like this for fun. He had formed this view some time ago and had no reason to alter it.

For Kate's take on this savoy dinner, she saw it as male pride being deflated, but she was sad all the same. That was the bit that frightened her, she knew that she was falling for this detective and couldn't just let it go. She was aware of her patrician airs and mocking tones, but like most girls, thought that the target of all these feminine "devices," this poor defenceless male, would take it in good humour and rebound and come good.

What many women don't know, especially the privileged few like Kate, is that the male ego is all the armour that most men have, and repeated bruising is sure to bear a price.

Yet Kate was savvy enough to note that — ego apart — Harry wasn't like most men in a still male-domineering society. She saw and liked the way he demurred to Milly, bearing her barbs nicely enough. He saw how he liked and respected Sarah Gately, and yet not her when she was in a playful mood with him. She figured that this was because he might be falling in love with her, and this could be the reason for the touchiness. He was gauche, but she meant it in the nicest way, inexperienced would be more accurate, but then so was she. Kate had the presence of mind to surmise that two things stood in their way, Harry's resistance to commit to her while she was engaged to her cousin, and his obvious reluctance to try to breach the class barrier. She would put all this aside for the present but come back to it when she next crossed paths, or swords, with Harry. But she counselled herself that playing with fire is a dangerous game and she could only push him so far. She was honest enough to tell herself that what she really wanted was for Harry to pull her into his arms and kiss her, often!

CHAPTER 8
Dr Jedidiah Leland

Harry spent the next week in a sullen mood and steeled himself against any more emotions or potential episodes with Kate. The weekend came and he decided to drive up to the cottage to see Milly. Jim was there for lunch and all three rustled about as close friends do, then after lunch, Jim and Milly sat arm-in-arm on the settee while Harry related all that had passed at Sarah's flat. Both took it in, nodding now and then, and agreeing that the next step was to find Dr Leland. Milly would wait for Jim and Harry to do their searches then report back to her and Kate. Milly walked Jim out to his car, exchanging kisses, and then off he drove to Wilcote Hall.

Closing the door behind her, Milly fixed a stern gaze at Harry, 'Idiot!'

'So, you've heard about the Savoy dinner! Look, sis, I love you dearly, but this is not your business.'

'Damn hell it is when it involves my brother and soon-to-be sister-in-law! She knows how much you like her, and she feels the same but doesn't want to commit while she is still engaged to her cousin.'

'So why did she invite me up to her room, after paying the bill herself, as if that wasn't a stab to the ribs? Bet she didn't tell you about that, eh!'

'Yes, she did, and she was crying as she did so. She was in two minds, caught between two men, and only wanted you to share another drink in her room and mess around a bit, but not, if I can put it politely, in the biblical sense. We girls have feelings too, yes, even cold, stuck-up girls, but Kate is no such type. Oh, I thought her cold and distant at first, but not now, knowing her as I do. She holds back, needs to be sure, is savvy and smart, but feels emotions like everyone else, and is very inexperienced in dealing with men. Surely you noticed, Harry. No, don't answer, I've had to put up with your failed romances for the past few years.'

She went on, 'I hope you feel like a heel. I expect Kate will now put the shutters down and give you that cold fish exterior you seem to expect and like from her! Didn't it occur to you that this was new territory for her as well? She doesn't dine and stay at the Savoy every week you know. With all that wealth and all those hyphenated names, she is still flesh and blood like the rest of us.'

Harry was staring at a crumb on the rug during his sister's dressing down. Then he looked up and said,

'Sis, you're right, I am a heel, and I've messed this up badly. But she'll go on to marry her cousin and that's the end of it.'

After a long pause while they both cleared the table, Harry spoke, 'Let's try to enjoy the rest of the weekend. Then I'll torture myself by diving back into my murder mystery.'

The telephone rang a little later. It was Jim inviting Milly and Harry to the Hall for afternoon drinks, dinner, and Sunday lunch. Milly didn't even ask Harry, instead accepted for both with alacrity. Harry had been chastened enough not to argue, so within the hour, off they drove to the Hall. For some years now, and especially after the war, it looked like time would no longer stand still for the idle rich and landed gentry. Here at Wilcote, the trend seemed afoot at the comforting and comfortable greetings each time Milly and Harry came to the Hall. They were met in the drive; big hugs for Milly from the whole family and handshakes all round for Harry.

When it came to Kate's turn, she stared beyond Harry's eyes, but taking his sister's chastisement and his own feeling of guilt, he captured Kate's attention with,

'So happy to see you again, cousin, twice-removed.' She forced a smile, he mouthed, "sorry" softly and the smile stretched a little further. Kate sensed, knew, that Milly had dressed down her brother severely. Nothing other than an apology would do and he gave it. Harry had been berated like a misbehaving child, but Kate took no solace from it, she too was feeling guilty. She was aware that his take on her mischievous deeds was that she had toyed with his feelings and treated him as an inferior, a plaything for her to enjoy in her free time, while she dithered with her own emotions. That was not her intention, but it was what it must surely have looked like to Harry.

Kate could only recall crying once or twice since childhood, so her tears at the Savoy, and later in relating the events to Milly, told her that she was sailing into uncharted waters.

The group went up the stairs and into the hall. Idle chatter all round for the remainder of Saturday until the conclusion of dinner when the erstwhile "Oxford Four" was rocked by Dexter's announcement that another guest would be arriving for lunch Sunday, a Dr Jedidiah Leland, whom he believed was at the recent engagement party. The "Four" stole furtive glances at one another and as they were leaving the table, decided to gather in the billiards room for a quick discussion.

Harry led off, 'Jim and I were about to search for this Dr Leland and lo, here he is turning up to lunch tomorrow! We figured that the doctor had somehow procured an invite to the engagement party, but this tells us something else entirely. What is his connection here? Jim?'

'Just as surprised as you, old man. I'm sure it's something very simple like Dexter making a new friend of him at the party and thinking it a good idea to ask him round.'

'Yes, that seems plausible,' yielded Milly, while Kate nodded silently.

'Tomorrow is looming as an important day in this case,' ended Jim.

As they moved to the door, Harry took Kate's arm and kept her from leaving. 'I'd like to apologise more formally and regret being awful to you the other night. I'd like to wish you the best for your future.'

'Thank you, Harry. We should put those events behind us. So, no regrets?'

'Only one.'

'Oh, what is it?' said Kate, half fearing a reproval of sorts.

'The only regret I have is not going with you to your room at the Savoy. Just my luck, first ever visit to the Savoy with a peach of a girl and I storm off in a huff. Milly called me an idiot for treating you so badly and she was right.' He looked at her and caught her mischievous rejoinder,

'Bright girl, that Milly.'

'How does a mere mortal man, nay idiot, deal with two clever women? Good night, Kate.'

'Good night, Harry.'

Both parted with the same thought in their minds. Each wanted to grab the other in a warm embrace but dared not in realising that it wouldn't be going anywhere.

Sunday arrived with clouds and rain. Fires were lit and breakfast came and went without much new except for one short conversation between Helen and Harry.

Both had moved to a window to watch the rain and the drops rasping on the glass like little explosions.

Helen spoke first, 'You must be wondering Harry why we have warmed so much to your Milly?'

'You mean to speak of the class difference, Mrs Wilson-Smythe.'

'No, not that, and I would like you to call me Helen.'

'Yes of course… Helen.'

'Richard and I are so very happy for Jim. I know you and he are now the best of friends, but the only way class comes into this situation is when Dexter inherits the estate. Dexter is a bit of a loner, you know. Richard and I have spoken a couple of times about how pretty and clever your sister is, but inside, there is a warm, caring, courteous and lovely girl very much in love with Jim as he is with her. It's an ulterior motive, I know, but we'd like a male heir, and it is looking less than likely that Dexter will ever take us in that direction.'

'Helen, it's very kind of you to say that about Milly. She is the best sister and puts me in my place when I need it.' He was still smarting from her recent withering temper at his treatment of Kate.

'I'm glad you said that Harry. Jim has been spoiled, so he will need the same medicine, I'm sure.'

Dr Leland arrived to be greeted outside by Dexter, then by the others at pre-lunch drinks. He was an amiable looking man, late-forties, medium height, cherubic face. At lunch, he joined in the general conversations around the table and afterwards, with the others, walked out onto a covered terrace to watch the rain, now teeming down.

'Frightful weather,' Jim said to Dr Leland who could only nod in agreement. 'By the way, doctor, have you heard of the case Harry and I are running presently?'

Without the slightest betrayal of emotion, he replied, 'A little, from Dexter, when he came down to London a week or so ago. It seems an odd business.'

'Yes, it surely is, doctor, and Harry and I are at our wits' end to crack it. I expect the Chief Super to relieve us of it any day now.'

'Oh, really, that will be a shame, a capital case taken out of your hands.'

Harry moved nearer, and asked, 'Doctor, have you ever heard of a Charles Fitzroy Keane, or a Daphne Welles.'

Dr Leland's eyes squinted, as he said, 'No, can't say that either of those names are familiar. Oh, wait up, isn't Keane the man in your case, the one who was killed in Cornwall?'

'Yes, but you've never met him or his *daughter* Daphne?' Harry had deliberately related the two to see if it raised a reaction from Leland.

He did pause momentarily, before saying: 'You say daughter, but their last names are different.'

'Yes, doctor, but not that rare, she might have been his step-daughter, or a legal name change, but the relationship is certain, we have the evidence.'

This caught him off-guard without comment and he wished them the best, hoping that the Chief Super would allow them more slack on the case, then excusing himself, walked over to Dexter and Richard.

The doctor left soon after. Jim managed to prise Dexter away from the others and asked him about Dr Leland, when and how they'd met and how well did he know the doctor. Soon after, the now "Wilcote Four" gathered in the billiards room for the boys to appraise Kate and Milly of their joust with Dr Leland, and for Jim to tell them that Dexter only met Dr Leland a few months ago at his club in London but that they had struck up a friendship which led to the invitation to the engagement party, where he introduced him to the family. A lot had happened in a short couple of conversations! Dexter's explanation was plausible, but the doctor's involvement with CFK and Daphne Welles at St Kevin's sanitorium was one hell of a coincidence to reckon with.

Milly exclaimed, 'Dr Leland's life might now be in peril by virtue of his being at the party with Brogan-Moore, and probably being introduced. Brogan-Moore could easily follow up with his own enquiries and find a link to CFK and Daphne. You two detectives will have to organise protection for him.'

'Not really,' said Kate, 'Brogan-Moore has only just met Dr Leland and there is little chance of his associating the doctor with CFK and even were he to do so, why should Dr Leland be any sort of threat to Brogan-Moore?'

'Yes, Kate, right you are,' added Milly. 'So, what's next?'

No one had anything to add until Harry spoke up, 'You know, it must be difficult to hide three living persons under disguised names and two of them now dead.'

'It's frustrating,' added Jim, 'there are no matching records and short of bringing Leland and Brogan-Moore to The Yard for questioning, that both would easily evade, we might have to leave it to settle for a while, or until the Chief Super decides we are not making enough progress.'

The others nodded reluctantly, and the weekend ended as it began, with Jim, Harry, and Milly driving back to Oxford and London.

Try as they could, Harry and Jim had no success in uncovering any relevant information on Dr Leland. Nor did they expect to, given his disguised name. So, it came as a shock the next day when Dexter called Jim from his club to say that Dr Leland had just taken ill at the club and was pronounced dead on arrival at St Thomas's hospital in Whitechapel. Was Milly right after all? Feminine intuition had taken great strides in this case so far, and was seemingly taking another leap forward.

Jim told Harry what he had feared since the engagement party. 'Here we are now with three dead people, all with disguised names and yet only one seems to have been murdered. And none of them had identification papers or an address, except for Dr Leland having rooms to treat patients, but where he lived was unknown. Harry, old man, there must be something we've missed?'

'Yes, it's all so mystifying. We might have to see the Chief Super.'

When the news of Dr Leland's death reached Milly and Kate a few days later, both girls spoke about it on the telephone and then Milly called Jim at his office. She asked him to tell Harry that the odds were against these three deaths not being suspicious and only one avenue was left open to the group.

The next day, Harry booked a meeting with Chief Superintendent Sinclair at which he asked permission to exhume two graves, those of Daphne Welles *and* Dr J Leland. The Chief said that this was highly irregular given that nothing seemed amiss in formal reports when these two died and were pronounced ready for burial. Welles died of tuberculosis and Leland, seemingly, of a heart attack. Nevertheless, Harry insisted that the exhumations were the only course left to follow. The Chief Super agreed, reluctantly, and arranged the permission papers to be taken to the respective cemetery registries.

As Harry grabbed the door handle to let himself out, he turned back to check with the Chief Super on something that was off to one side of his mind, but that kept bothering him.

'If I could trouble you for another few minutes, Chief, something has been gnawing at me for some time now.'

'Yes, what is it, my boy?'

'Sir, I've been worried about the coincidences in this case.'

'What coincidences?'

'Well, when Jim was posted on the case with me, who'd have expected that the Wilson-Smythes just happen to be involved in this business, albeit indirectly through Jim's older brother, Dexter.'

'Go on.'

Sir, don't you see it as odd that I'm thrown in with Jim and then I meet his mysterious brother who is vague about his meetings with Brogan-Moore and Dr Leland?'

'Yes, Harry, a coincidence, for sure. Is that all?'

Harry looked nonplussed. 'Sir...' He was stopped in his tracks by the Chief Super's next utterance.

'Harry, we have coincidences in many cases and this one falls neatly under that umbrella. Is it just a coincidence, or *could* it be something more sinister, and as with just about all such instances, it will reveal which it is in due course? Look, you young pups haven't been around as long as I have to see crime at work and the delicate tendrils of clues in all directions. Coincidences abound in our world, indeed just look at crime fiction — try reading Arthur Conan Doyle or Agatha Christie.'

He went on, 'Let me give you a simple example. You leave home at eight a.m. and take the train into Central London. On this train trip, you meet, by happenstance, a couple of people, one of whom is from your native Ireland, a pretty girl you'd like to take to lunch, which you do. Track forward to when you eventually marry, and your life direction is set. Now, if on that same day, you had left home at eight-thirty a.m., that event wouldn't have happened, but other events could have, or perhaps nothing at all. Two entirely and wildly different outcomes. Say you went to a different school, or on a different holiday, your future changes with each event as it unfolds in your present comings and goings. These things are all around us and we rarely take the time to notice. Coincidences are events that drive life forward. In crime, they always seem puzzling, odd, or sinister, but there they are.'

'Thank you, sir. I hadn't thought about it like that.'

On he went to meet Jim for lunch. Afterwards, they arranged for pathologists attached to Scotland Yard to examine the exhumed bodies. A few days later, the doctor in London sent a report from the government laboratory to the Chief Super, who passed it on to his young detectives, with a note asking them to move forward with haste.

When they read the report, out jumped the statement that *strychnine* had been detected in Dr

Leland's blood. Murder number two was added to their burden. Someone had gotten at Dr Leland at Dexter's club, and since Dexter was an unlikely poisoner, it must have been Brogan-Moore or his "envoy." The news was telephoned through to their sisters, then all four waited with dread for the second report.

When it came two days later, it was very brief. It stated that *no* remains were found in the coffin at St Mark's cemetery. Daphne Welles not only had a false name, but she might never have existed!' All four were astonished.

The group needed time to take this in and to plan their next move. What about her death certificate? Forged, of course, but why was Dr Leland at St Kevin's sanitorium that day? And what about the records of her two years of illness at the sanitorium? The only item that was still tangible in their minds was the only survivor left standing in this case, William Brogan-Moore MP.

CHAPTER 9
Lavinia and the *Wilcote Cell*

Kate visited Milly about a week later. They lunched at a café in Oxford. Kate looked even less talkative than her usual self, prompting Milly to ask, 'Kate, is anything troubling you?'

'Dear Milly, thank you for your concern, but nothing I'd like to talk about.'

'I can be a good listener,' pressed Milly. 'Did anything more happen between you and my addle-headed brother?'

''No, no, he apologised, and we settled on a friendly distance. But tell me one thing, Milly, am I a fool to marry my cousin?'

'Only if you don't love him,' came back the obvious answer.

'Yes,' said Kate looking at her plate while prodding at the mostly uneaten food with her fork.'

'Do you have *any* feelings for Harry?' ventured Milly.

Kate smiled, half laughed, 'Do you recall all those times when I was cool and aloof to him?'

'Yes, of course, it was impossible not to notice. At the time, I thought — and forgive me for this — that you were patrician in your ways and turned your nose up at this very awkward pup who was trying to get you to like him.'

'No need to apologise, Milly, my nose turns up quite often! But what if I told you that I fell for your brother the first time I met him at the Hall.'

Milly gulped audibly. 'What?'

'Naturally, I baulked at this impossible duet but had wilted completely by the time we had dinner at the Savoy. I wouldn't know what love was if it hit me in the face, but every time I saw Harry, I had butterflies in my stomach and went a bit light in the head and tried my best to assume the indifferent posture of an upright cadaver!'

This caused Milly to giggle as Kate went on, 'My patrician icy airs can be turned on and off on a whim and I was doing my best to hide my feelings in fear of Harry not liking *me*. But I couldn't resist. When I kissed him, I was gone. The problem was in trying to gauge if he felt the same. But it didn't work because of my engagement to my cousin, Ralph. Harry thought that I was only after a fling to entertain myself until the wedding. I needed time to make things right but then we all became so involved with this case that I set my feelings aside, hoping it would all come good in the end.'

'Gosh, that's a new one on me. I would never have guessed, and neither would, Harry, poor dear. You can be assured that I'll not say anything to him. Harry is a gentleman and will keep his distance because he can't believe that your feelings are genuine. The next step, if there is to be one, is up to you.'

'Thanks, Milly, you are a dear.' The girls hugged each other and went out into the sunshine.

The "Wilcote Four" met at the Hall the next weekend. Jim and Milly continued their little romantic interludes around the rest of the family gatherings for tea, lunch, and dinner. Lavinia begged Kate to allow her to join them for their meeting this weekend.

'How ghoulish, little sister, are you sure you want to bring this tragic stuff into your life? You should be off looking for a suitable future husband, my sweet,' said Kate, brushing a hand across her sister's cheek.

'Odd of you to say that Kate, I have a terrible business to tell you — I've been seeing cousin Ralph, for some time now and he is steeling himself to face father to ask him permission to transfer his affection from you to me. After all, you've hardly talked to him or met him these past few months.'

Kate peered into the distance and said, half to herself as to her sister, 'You know, I never did warm to mother's wish for us to marry and I can assure you that I never fell in love with Ralph. It's no surprise that you have become close. Lavinia dear, you have just made me realise my indolence and lack of emotion towards myself for the first time. Saying it out loud here has convinced me that I haven't been fair to Ralph, but now that the two of you have found a bond, I wish you both the best!'

'Oh, thank you, Kate, I was so scared of you finding out,' as she kissed her older sister's cheek.

Kate thought to herself that she had escaped her engagement without a single word or deed on her part! As they walked along to the meeting, Kate smiled and said to herself, "Cousin, once-removed has been removed!" She then thought of a very apt parallel with Harry's rogue compatriot, Oscar Wilde. She mouthed to herself the clever way in which Oscar Wilde would have put it, "To lose one cousin may be regarded as a misfortune; to lose two looks like carelessness!"

Back to the present situation, 'Now, about that meeting Lavinia, still want to come along.'

'Yes.'

So it was that the five met that afternoon to talk of murder and a missing body and of their gathering suspicion that Brogan-Moore was involved. Lavinia listened intently while the four "detectives" ran through the evidence and the actions that were needed to close out this case. Lavinia, all innocent and ignorant in the ways of the world, was showing signs of fear and sadness, as tears welled against her best efforts to stop them.

'Oh dear, I knew this might happen, I shouldn't have let you join us,' bemoaned Kate.

'Yes, of course, bad idea,' said Harry.

Lavinia composed herself, wiped away the beginnings of tears, then looked around the table at what she now realised would become her inquisitors when she blurted out, 'None of you know what happens in dark corners, in lonely places when older men try to take advantage of young girls.'

This was a shock, but before anyone could speak, Lavinia continued, 'When war broke out, father and mother moved into the village and you two were away at school. Dexter and I were left here in the small cottage behind the Hall to look after things. Kate, Jim, don't you recall how Wilcote Hall was given over to a small *Cell* for intelligence gathering and assisting decoders?'

'Yes,' said Jim, 'but that finished years ago.'

'Not all of it,' said Lavinia ominously. 'Some of those men were fiends. I recall more than once being approached and propositioned for you-know-what and touched and almost mauled quite a few times.'

'Why didn't you tell father or mother,' implored Kate.

'Why, because our brother, Dexter, was one of them! How could I tell them that. Oh, he wasn't brave enough to maul the victims, just the provider or silent partner for the others' pleasures. And he protected me most of the time.' All four listeners were aghast and open-mouthed as this news came out of this innocent's mouth.

Lavinia continued, 'There were two who were part of this ring, respectable MP William Brogan-Moore, and Dr Jedidiah Leland. When they both turned up at the engagement party, I thought that I would die. Silly Dexter had no idea how it would affect me. I kept out of sight thinking that one or both might recognise me, or worse, try to entice Dexter to become provider again, but he never came near me. I think that all three have a sort of hold over each other and they bob up now and then to massage egos and toast their good fortune in having escaped being exposed.'

Harry butted in, 'So, that's the connection between those two. They knew each other from their time here during the war, and yet pretended to be strangers at the engagement party.'

Jim spoke, 'Lavinia, this is terrible, but it must end in justice, even if it means Dexter being arrested and sent to prison. Leland is gone and will bother no one any more, and Brogan-Moore will pay his dues soon enough.'

'Dexter never touched me or the other girls, thank God, but he knew what the others were trying to do to me and the other girls staying here out of harm's way – that's a laugh. We were thirteen, fourteen or fifteen. Who would believe girls of that age accusing respectable men of reprehensible deeds?'

'This is morbid in the extreme,' added Milly.

'You poor little thing,' said Kate cradling her sister. 'It's all right now that it has come out.'

'I feel a great burden lifting. To be honest, I don't know how I would have continued to cope without

Ralph's close attention these past months. Don't worry, I haven't told anyone about this business before today. Nor will I ever, unless compelled to do so if these events ever need to be recalled.'

CHAPTER 10
The "Wilcote Four" Meet for the Last Time

Kate walked Lavinia out of the room and returned in time to hear Jim speaking.

'We've got a real mess on our hands here. There were fiends among the innocents. How many others were stained by this cabal? Dexter might have been a silent partner, but he must have derived some evil pleasure from knowing what was happening. Heaven forbid, he may even have been present, or a participant, at some of these terrible events.'

'Conspirator, yes,' said Kate, 'but participant, no. I know Dexter too well. He is a lonely figure, with no purpose in life, and no ambition, he has never drifted far from mother's skirts. He may have morbid or perverse desires, but his pleasure in all of this comes from being an observer, never a risk-taker. He has always suffered from boredom and inertia and this can do crazy things to the mind, especially when you have others around you of similar thinking, but having no qualms about actively pursuing their perversions.'

'What makes you so sure, Kate,' said Jim, half hoping she was right about Dexter being only a silent member of the *Wilcote Cell*.

'I too suffer from indolence in this place, day after day, nothing happens, but a few years ago, I took to making trips to the Bodleian and became an avid reader. One topic which gained my attention was the many books on psychology and psychoses. It's in these books that I've read about the Dexters, the Brogan-Moores, and the Lelands of this world. And you know, it frightened me out of having normal feelings for others. Emotion, romance, and companionship became anathema to me, and my character hardened. I stopped reading those books a few months ago, then Milly and Harry came along and I was jealous of your normalcy, your easy manner, yes, even your social clumsiness. I watched as Jim caught all of this and became one of you. I wanted to join in, but it took courage that I didn't have, that is, until I met an idiot and took him to dinner at the Savoy.'

Milly and Jim laughed but Harry just looked at Kate who went on,

'Well, cousin, twice-removed, what do you think of me now?'

Harry drew himself up, looked at Milly and then at Jim, both beginning little smiles back to him.

'Kate, this little speech of yours is the first time I've seen you vulnerable,' then surprised all three when he added, 'but you know, I liked your implacable patrician icy exterior, your surly ways, your dismissive looks. It suits you admirably, and makes you look even more attractive.'

Kate looked up at him, smiled and mouthed silently, 'Thank you, Harry.'

Meanwhile, Milly was distracted distilling the events that had just passed between them concerning Dexter and Lavinia, and she injected, 'There is no doubt that Brogan-Moore knew Dr Leland here at the Hall during the war and probably through him, found out years later about Charles Fitzroy Keane. Brogan-Moore couldn't have CFK pottering around and asking questions about Daphne's stay here during the war. CFK's death warrant was stamped and issued for that cold dark night in West Cornwall. That brings us to Brogan-Moore, who must have killed or arranged to have killed Dr Leland. So, to sum up, we have two problems to solve. One, where is the evidence to convict Brogan-Moore? Two, where is Daphne Welles?'

'Perfect summing up, sis. It was easy for Leland to "adopt" a recent corpse and produce a death certificate to satisfy the authorities. Dr Leland went ahead with the burial, not of their surrogate corpse, whose separate burial justified his falsifying of the death certificate, but of an empty coffin for Daphne's gravesite. His idea was to protect CFK's daughter, Daphne, who was probably bundled off to Scotland or Australia, or some such place to try to lead a normal life, under her real name which would not be known to the fiends back here. In this way, he believed that CFK and he too would also be protected by this subterfuge.'

Jim's turn came as he said, 'Our missing girl, Daphne, is now safe. Nothing happened after the war until 1948 when Brogan-Moore became suspicious, from what source of information we are yet to determine. CFK had to be silenced if he was told everything about the *Cell* by Dr Leland, whose complicity in assisting CFK marked him for an early death. I'm not sure how much of this Dexter knows, but he is the key to settling this case. I'm sure we will hook Brogan-Moore once Dexter tells all he knows.'

All sighed audibly at these dastardly details as they went to their rooms. All would be settled in the next few days, or so they hoped.

CHAPTER 11
The End of Inspector Dillon's First Case

Chief Superintendent Douglas Sinclair turned up at Wilcote Hall on a bleak Monday morning. He thought it only proper to attend in view of the importance of the Wilson-Smythes in the community. Also, there was the delicate matter of one of his investigating detectives being the second son in the family. Jim and Harry met him in a spare drawing room and appraised him of all the details, with the purpose of confronting Dexter and making his arrest for complicity in the *Wilcote Cell* and its evil practices.

While the Chief Super waited in the drawing room now with Dexter, the "Wilcote Four" tried to be as tactful as possible in relating the dire events of this case and Dexter's role in the *Cell* to his parents. Lavinia was spared this difficult episode by being bundled off to an aunt in the next county. Richard and Helen were shocked, grief-stricken, and speechless. It was clear to Jim and Kate that their parents would never truly recover from this tragedy. Harry tried his best to console them with the prospect of Dexter serving only a short sentence for complicity, especially if he co-operated fully with the police.

It began, more or less as the "Four" had surmised. Many of their "facts" were guesses, but they were good guesses. The rest would be on Dexter to fill in the gaps, which he proceeded to do, truthfully, as he had promised to the Chief Super. Dexter related how the intelligence *Cell* thought of themselves amongst the brightest in the land. Away from the fighting, and safely bottled up in the Hall brought many long weeks and months of plodding effort with the expected exhaustion and boredom during their free time. They were only allowed to travel to the local village and then for only short visits. None ever used their real names, so it was part of the subterfuge to make up names for themselves, protected by the "Official Secrets Act."

The vacuity of time and their narcissistic tendencies brought forward the cabal as the brainchild of Brogan-Moore, Dr Leland, and two others, who had since died. Dexter was recruited to organise 'subjects' for the *Cell*, some obliging, some not completely so. They came and went at the whim of the *Cell* members. Lavinia, young and innocent, and suspecting nothing, went among the boffins, mingling occasionally until their unwanted advances began. Dexter was attentive enough to shield her from the excesses of these men, keeping her away most of the time.

When there was a shortage of subjects, a dastardly plan was hatched. Dr Leland could bring his school friend's daughter to stay for a few weeks under cover of introducing her to country estate living. She went by the name Daphne Welles, and no one bothered to ask if it was her real name. She never returned to her father. He was given the terrible news by his friend, Dr Leland, that she had come down with tuberculosis and was bundled off to St Kevin's sanitorium, where she would remain in isolation. But did she die? She wasn't at her gravesite, and even Dexter was at pains to figure what had really happened to her. She might have recovered and be living elsewhere under her real name, just as the "Four" had surmised.

Dexter broke down when he told the Super that he was ashamed of his part in the *Cell*, but in the ferocity of war and its temporal fleeting uncertainty, he was driven to distraction and disgrace, abandoning all he believed in or cherished, even allowing his sister to be "handled" by these men. Dexter told the Chief Super how Brogan-Moore had recently co-opted and commissioned Dr Leland to find his old school friend and have him killed so that CFK would never find out the truth about his daughter's abuse at the Hall during the war.

'Leland told me at my club one afternoon when he had had too much scotch, that he carried out Brogan-Moore's "request" on that dark stormy night in West Cornwall. He found a local criminal and paid him to kill CFK. Of course, Dr Leland's days were now numbered. It was Brogan-Moore who had the most to lose with his political career, and it was he who must have poisoned Dr Leland. Brogan-Moore assured me that my demise was never to be an issue. He had insurance in that direction, in my cowardice to not reveal any of those dark events and worse, on the threat of arranging to kill our Lavinia. That's it, Chief Superintendent, I'd like to leave now.'

After the police and Dexter left, the rest of the family, with Harry and Milly, had drinks mostly in silence, only uttering snippets of small talk. The next day, they gathered in the morning room to continue soothing one another's grief from the previous day.

Harry stood up and announced that they still had an unsolved murder. The others gave him puzzled looks. Was there a sensational twist that no one had yet suspected?

'But Harry,' said Jim, 'we know about CFK and Dr Leland, both dead. Brogan-Moore will be arrested tomorrow. Daphne is safe somewhere or other. What are you saying?'

Harry went on, 'What I'm saying is that we have been dealing with demons in Dr Leland and Brogan-Moore and their two now-departed conspirators in this child molesting *Cell*. Lavinia was saved from the worst of their perversions because Dexter was reluctant to give her over to those men. But what about the other three or four girls and Daphne?'

Kate chimed in, giving Harry his official title, 'Inspector, I've read quite a bit about this type of sordid business and there is usually no real mystery to it, other than that the abused and mentally-damaged children block it out of their minds, or for fear of not being believed, or of being sent away to some unhappy boarding school or orphanage to mull over their ruined lives.'

Helen added, 'I've even heard of that happening in one instance years ago from a close friend who was herself abused when she was ten or eleven, but she swore me to never reveal her name or recount what happened to her. Now thirty-eight, she had just come out of a second failed marriage and was emigrating to Canada to start a new life.'

'All of that is well and good as far as it goes,' Harry again, 'but not this time. I was holding this back as the events of the last two days played out.'

He had their attention as he continued, 'Just a few days ago, my friend, Sarah, invited me up for tea and cake and we got to talking about the case again. She has been a great help, as we all know. Indeed, we may never have solved this case without her. Sarah convinced me that it was Dr Leland, not CFK, who devised the *Citizen Kane* disguises, and CFK's home village of Massinone. It had to be because when Dr Leland turned up here during the war to join the *Cell*, he needed to protect himself from being discovered and uncovered as a fiend. When they were starved of subjects, and Dexter realised the threat to Lavinia, it was Dexter who told us yesterday that Dr Leland would procure his friend's daughter, Daphne Welles.'

'Sarah also worked out that Leland would be savvy enough to protect his friend and daughter if something went wrong later. His friend became CFK who lived in Massinone, and the daughter became Daphne Welles. As the *Cell* would never know about CFK, Daphne could easily be disguised as "Welles." She didn't die, was never interred at St Mark's, and was bundled off to another country.'

'So far, you've told us nothing really new, Harry, other than that Leland was the *Citizen Kane* name organiser and not CFK,' said Milly.

'Yes, sis, but now comes the clincher. Sarah asked me to go over everything we knew about the doctor and especially to recount any exchanged conversation. Well, this was difficult, and I couldn't venture anything at first but then I recalled Dexter tagging me at the engagement party for a minute or so. I asked him how he came to know Dr Leland and he gave me the story about his club in London. Then he said something that I thought of no consequence at the time and didn't think it worth mentioning, but out it came when Sarah and I met the other day.'

'I remembered Dexter asking me if I ever went skiing, to which I replied "never," for fear of breaking my neck. He then mentioned Dr Leland being an avid skier since childhood.' Dexter went on to say, 'He has a childhood sled mounted on the wall of his consulting room in London. I recall seeing it there. Well, that did it for Sarah, our astute film buff.'

She lit up saying, 'Harry there must be something in that snippet of gossip about Dr Leland. You wouldn't know that in *Citizen Kane*, Charles Foster Kane was taken from his parents, adopted really, by a rich banker, who remunerated the parents handsomely from a silver mine licence they had but couldn't develop without the banker's help. The banker took the young Kane with him, and he was sent to the best schools, for he was to inherit all that wealth when he reached adulthood. The only thing that Kane took with him was his sled, which had a name painted on the top. This must be the last piece in the *Citizen Kane* puzzle,' she announced emphatically. 'Now how does it fit into this case?' She answered her own question, 'Ah, I know,' Sarah exclaimed. 'Harry, you must prepare yourself for yet another shock in this horrible business.'

Harry continued, 'It was an unconnected final clue, until now. Sarah came up with the most probable solution. I kept this back yesterday to allow the grief about Dexter to run its course.'

Harry then recounted the mystery in *Citizen Kane*, as told to him by Sarah, 'The sled was the only thing that Kane took with him when sent away to boarding school, but we don't know its significance until the end of the film, after Kane dies. You see, the name on the sled was hidden under Kane's arm when he was whisked away by the banker. An old warehouse was packed with a lifetime of mostly worthless memorabilia that Kane had accumulated. It was sorted and the worthless items were thrown into a raging furnace. One such item was Kane's childhood sled, and we see the name *Rosebud* just as it is thrust into the furnace. Sarah told me that Dr Leland had begun the *Citizen Kane* disguises to protect himself, his friend CFK, and Daphne, insurance against Brogan-Moore, if you like, against retribution or blackmail. So too he devised the final clue of the sled.'

Helen broke in, 'But Harry, why is this of any relevance now, the case is over isn't it?'

'Not quite, Helen. I might be clutching at nothing here, but can I ask you and Richard when you planted out your rose garden?'

Helen answered, 'We didn't. The men who commandeered the Hall for their war work started it themselves as a gift of thanks for letting them use our home.'

'Then I must brace you all for a shock. We will have to dig up the rose garden, which we all know is a rich source of... *rosebuds*. This was Leland's last clue, his supposed insurance against Brogan-Moore.'

'Dr Leland must have duped his friend, Charles Fitzroy Keane, by telling him that he could visit Daphne at the sanitorium, where she was taken after coming down ill during her stay here. But close access would be denied for fear of infection. Leland would take CFK to a ward, and from behind a glass panel, look at a girl in a bed across the room. She was an unknown waif for whom Dr Leland managed to provide papers identifying her as Daphne Welles, but it wasn't her! He had hidden the secret from his friend.'

'Daphne was apparently "buried" at St Mark's, but we now know that the site was bogus. Leland's elaborate scheme of disguise and counter-disguise was meant to dupe CFK *and* Brogan-Moore, and to protect himself. It was only after he had pangs of conscience that he disclosed this "real" gravesite to CFK earlier this year, which prompted CFK's visit to St Mark's, which started this whole mess. Leland would have told CFK to be wary and careful in searching out his daughter's gravesite, and this explains his night-time visit. Poor soul, even that didn't protect him, but he'd been warned, hence the puzzle.'

'Back in 1948, Dr Leland had probably told CFK that Daphne had to be cremated due to the risk of disease, which indeed is the usual practice, and CFK accepted his friend's explanation, that is, until Leland recanted and told his friend that his daughter was buried at St Mark's. Brogan-Moore must have had Leland under close surveillance, which explains how he came to find CFK at Muirford. I've already asked the Yard to send out a team and they will be here tomorrow morning with a police pathologist.'

'Oh god, no,' exclaimed Helen, the others dumbstruck, as she continued, 'Are you saying that Daphne was brought here, abused, and killed by those men after she threatened to expose their practices, and then was buried in our rose garden?'

'Sadly, that is my unfortunate suspicion,' said Harry. 'The fiendish Dr Leland had to cover it up with the St Mark's gravesite lest his friend CFK become suspicious. The most obvious explanation is that, as you've said, Helen, Daphne may have rebelled, resisted, and threatened to go to the police, and so had to be killed. These details should emerge from the Yard's interrogation of Brogan-Moore in the coming days.'

'I must insist that no one here be present when the police arrive tomorrow. I think it best if you arrange a local trip to Woodstock or Oxford until at least mid-afternoon.'

Tuesday unfurled cool and sunny, as a police team and pathologist arrived mid-morning. The garden was dug up systematically and carefully. After about an hour, a skeleton was uncovered, and the pathologist made a preliminary but confident statement that this was the skeleton of an adolescent female.

Harry's 'missing girl' had been found! Poor Daphne Welles, only sixteen, her real name still a mystery. Harry was astute and sensitive enough to organise the transfer of Daphne's remains to her proper gravesite at St Mark's cemetery. He also directed that the rose garden be levelled, and the site covered in new lawn that would meld with the surrounding grass. The Wilson-Smythes were relieved when they were told this. Milly, Kate, and Jim thanked Harry for his insightful summing up the previous day. He had collated all the clues and guesses of these past weeks into a studious solution to the last mystery — the fate of the missing girl Daphne Welles.

It was all over. No one enjoyed the next few days. There was more drinking than usual, as an elixir to deaden the sorrow of the recent events. Richard lost himself in his library and pipe, Jim and Milly were away from the others, sullen and pensive, Helen and Kate busied themselves with books, cooking, and chatter. Lavinia remained at her aunt's for a few more days.

Helen issued invitations for all to meet the next weekend at Wilcote Hall, with a view to putting all this bad business behind them. She consoled herself, as well as a mother could, that Lavinia was spared who-knows-what horrors, and Dexter, though complicit and evil in thought, was not by deed.

Harry was on his way, a successful conclusion to a baffling case, but he felt empty inside. Were all murder cases like this, ruined lives, sadness, evil?

Harry took the news back to his good "egg" Sarah. Chief Superintendent Sinclair was appraised with a carefully written and signed report and he thanked his two junior inspectors for a job well done. Case closed!

CHAPTER 12
Full Moon

Jim, Harry, and Milly drove up to the Hall on the next Saturday afternoon. The healing had begun, it seemed, through good wishes and small talk. Indeed, talk of the upcoming wedding was *plat du jour* at dinner.

Saturday night had arrived with a full moon. It looked ghostly. The steely white light bathed everything in a grey-white metallic sheen. Its appearance allowed Harry to reflect on his time at the Hall. Odd really, he thought to himself. Were it not a full moon he would hardly have cared, or noticed, but seeing it there made him think that this was probably inspiration for many; writers, poets, musicians, Satanic worshippers, ancient civilisations that considered it a god perhaps, lovers, seafarers, astronomers and so on.

After dinner, he went out onto a terrace and down to the moonlit lawn, where his steps produced tell-tale audible notes of dry leaves crackling under his shoes. He loved this sound and made a few circles on the lawn to enhance this little musical piece before looking up and seeing Kate on the terrace. In this silvery light, she truly looked like one of those Greek goddesses.

'Oh, hello, Kate, thought I'd take in the full moon.'

'Me too.' Then after a few seconds, 'tell me, Harry, why haven't you tried to kiss me lately?'

This didn't take him by surprise, he was ready for Kate's hot and cold emotions, and he wasn't going to fall for it again, but knowing now that the betrothal to her cousin was dissolved, was she sending him a signal that he was the next man in her life? Or was she still playing games with him? He decided not to risk it, and his response caught Kate off-guard:

'The moon shines bright. In such a night as this,
When the sweet wind did gently kiss the trees
And they did make no noise, in such a night
Troilus methinks mounted the Troyan walls
And sigh'd his soul towards the Grecian tents
Where Cressid lay that night.'

'Sounds like Shakespeare,' Kate said tentatively.

'Yes, it's from *The Merchant of Venice*. I always think of it when I see a full moon.'

'That's very romantic, cousin,' she whispered, as she moved in and kissed him, like last time, gently at first and then passionately.

He drew away knowing that this little interlude would only haunt him later. He wanted to love her, but surely it was a lost cause.

Kate drew back slightly, then spoke, 'How come you know so much about literature and the arts? Has it been a hobby of yours?'

'No, it comes from studying arts at Merton College at Oxford some years ago. When I completed my degree, I couldn't see myself making a life out of it. At that time, I had read most of Conan Doyle's Sherlock Holmes stories and so, here I am.'

'Well, Sherlock, I am impressed. Did your time at Oxford include music?'

'A little, not enough time to cover so many topics.'

'Pity, I love music and especially Mozart. Does that surprise you?'

'Not at all, Mozart was almost metronomic in his music, writing it down as it played in his head, never a note out of place, melodious tunes mixed in with his stiffness of beats, almost military in its cadences. I can see why you would like his music.'

'Thank you for the assessment. But this is odd. How do you know so much about Mozart's music if you never studied it?'

'Simple really, there were concerts every few days at Oxford, still are, and I managed to get to quite a few of them. And I like reading biographies of famous people.'

'So, you are a fan of Mozart after all, like me,' Kate gleamed at him.

'No. Oh, I like most of it, but Beethoven is my favourite by quite a distance.'

'Really, all that fire, confusion, *and* noise.'

'Yes, you're right. *Eroica*, his third symphony, was originally dedicated to Napoleon until he proclaimed himself emperor! Beethoven was aghast and deleted the dedication. But listening to that soaring symphony brings in all of Napoleon's grand ideas, the conquest of Europe, the defeats, and finally, exile. Beethoven managed it in this monumental symphony. It changed music forever. But he also wrote some of the most melodious tunes we know today.'

'Oh, I suppose.' She'd hatched a plan to test him out. Poetry was one thing, with his Byron and Shakespeare, but she sensed that she had trapped him here. She wondered if he really listened to all that Beethoven 'noise.'

'Come inside, Harry, I'd like to play you one of my favourite Mozart pieces.'

In they went, she sat him down on a settee and started the radiogram. Removing a record from the cabinet, she set it going, sat alongside Harry, and waited to see his reaction.

'Good choice, Kate, my favourite piece of music.'

She had him! 'But that's Mozart, Harry.'

'That's not Mozart, Kate, that is Beethoven's *Fifth Symphony in C Minor*.'

'Touché, Inspector, I give in.'

'That's all right, Kate, but how serendipitous of you to choose that piece.'

'Serendipity had nothing to do with it. Milly told me weeks ago about your favourite composer and favourite piece. *Et voila!*'

'If I weren't a gentleman, I'd put you across my knee and spank you.'

She snuggled up to him. 'Aren't I lucky? I've just avoided a terrible ordeal, but I hope that you are gentlemanly enough to kiss me if I ask you to?'

'Are we going to start this again?'

She muffled his words with her hand across his mouth and moved in and kissed him again and again.

He drew back and said, 'Milly told me that I made you cry on two occasions. Before you say anything, please just listen. Milly said that you wouldn't tell me because it would make you look vulnerable and very human. Well, now I know and knowing it hurt me deeply. I don't deserve you, Kate. I thought that you were playing me along, but I now know that isn't so. Crying has a way of looking innocent and defenceless. It reminded me of a quotation I read once, not Shakespeare or Byron, or even Wilde this time. It's from the Talmud, "Be careful if you make a woman cry. God counts her tears."'

'I like that, I like that very much.' Kate paused, then added, 'Cousin, if your quote is to be taken seriously, then you have made me shed God knows how many tears. Now we wouldn't want to upset Him, or worse, add to the count, would we? So, why don't you spend the next few minutes kissing me to correct some of the deficit?'

Harry did exactly that, pulling her gently into his arms and kissing her. She responded with a passion both had never seen before. Then Kate rose from their embrace, and said, 'Goodnight, cousin, twice-removed.'

Harry stared at the wall, kept listening to his Beethoven, and dreamt of the impossible. Jim and Milly came back in and the three of them had a last drink before retiring for the evening.

On Sunday afternoon it was time to go. 'Well, that wraps it up, friends, we will next meet at a certain wedding,' said Jim, as he and Milly walked out into the bright sunshine. Goodbyes were exchanged all round.

Harry went up to Kate. 'I suppose that's it, Kate. Look, we are really pleased that you helped on this case. I expect we'll see each other at the wedding. Goodbye.'

Kate looked even more aloof and distant than usual, which Harry used as a reason for his own abrupt farewell. He thought that their kissing session last night might be another one of her whimsical dalliances. Just as he resigned himself to more doubt, she surprised him with a request, 'Cousin dear, will you take me in your arms and kiss me goodbye?'

He felt sheepishly embarrassed but did as she'd asked. A warm embrace and a farewell kiss.

She said goodbye, shook hands, and turned to walk back up the stairs into the hall. Harry looked down at a small envelope she had pressed into his hand. He looked back at Kate as she turned around, and said, 'Don't read it until you get home.'

He climbed into his car and wondered about the note on the way back to London. Was it an invitation to visit Wilcote Hall again? Worst of all, he feared it was a final "what could have been" farewell.

When he reached his little flat, he opened the envelope, took out the note and pressed it out on the table. The neat cursive pen strokes read:

A cryptic puzzle for Inspector Harry Dillon. Hope you solve it soon! No cheating, no running to Milly's cryptographer. Kate.

Mi koolgin rof na tidio ot avhe drenin whit exnt sayutard ta eth vosay, elvo ekta

His hopes fell when he saw Kate's words about not seeking help. Maybe he could sneak upstairs to ask Sarah? Kate would never find out. He knew it would be dishonest, but what of it, it's probably just one last dig in the ribs. He looked at the words again. Maybe it's Latin, or Greek, or Welsh?

Then he did what he always did when there was a conundrum to solve. He put on the kettle, made tea, opened a small tin, removed a biscuit, and sat down to look at the scrambled letters on the scrap of paper. Four minutes, then 'Eureka!' He had worked it out. Not that hard after all as he smiled and spoke the words out loud:

"I'm looking for an idiot to have dinner with next Saturday at the Savoy. Love, Kate."